IAM THE EARTH THE PLANTS GROW THROUGH

.ll.

I AM THE EARTH THE PLANTS GROW THROUGH

a novel

JACK HANNAN

.II.

Prepared for the press by Katia Grubisic
Copyediting: Jennifer McMorran
Author photo: Molly Shea-Hannan
Cover design: Debbie Geltner
Cover image: Molly Shea-Hannan
Book design: Tika eBooks

Library and Archives Canada Cataloguing in Publication

Title: I Am the Earth the Plants Grow Through: a novel / Jack Hannan.
Names: Hannan, Jack, 1949 – author.
Identifiers: Canadiana (print) 20210187034 | Canadiana (ebook) 20210187042 |
ISBN 9781773900957 (softcover) | ISBN 9781773900964 (EPUB) |
ISBN 9781773900971 (Kindle) | ISBN 9781773900988 (PDF)
Classification: LCC PS8565.A585 I12 2021 | DDC C813/.S4-dc23

Printed and bound in Canada.

The publisher gratefully acknowledges the support of the Government of Canada through the Canada Council for the Arts, the Canada Book Fund, and the Government of Quebec through the Societé de développement des entreprises culturelles (SODEC).

Linda Leith Publishing
Montreal
www.lindaleith.com

To Deborah, Molly, Nick, Jesse, Katrina, Kai, Quinn, Miles, and Nesta.

"I would have chosen to have lost, among my memories, those of the self and the self's failures, and to have retained the memories of our lavish world."

—Anne Boyer

Prelude

Let me put you behind the wheel of a clean, rented automobile. You are driving on a highway between two cities. This is in Canada, and it will take a good part of the day to reach your destination. Your hosts will have dinner ready when you arrive. The speed limit is 100 kilometres per hour but you're going 118. The police seem willing to let anything go below 120. You are a relaxed and sensible person. There is a black Toyota Camry on the road about six car lengths ahead of you, with which you've fallen into a rhythm, travelling together over the last hour or so. You pass a lot of semis on the road and some clusters of cars, while other clusters pass you. There are a few people in that Toyota, but you are alone. You are on your way to visit friends. You have the radio turned up loud, and every few songs the station comes up with a good one for the road. *Get your motor running!* The music is loud and the windows are closed. It is easy to be swept away with the music, the trees passing along the side of the road. And you, on a line down the middle through fields and fields and fields.

At one point, more than halfway through your journey, another car draws up in the outside lane. It seems like it's going to pass you, but the driver is going about it very slowly. It's obvious he's using cruise control and he's set it at about 119 km per hour, only slightly faster than you. It takes him several long minutes to pass your car and you find this annoying, but you also will not slow down to let him pass more quickly. Why should you? He is beside you for a long time, inching ahead of your car as the two of you speed along. It feels oddly like an invasion of your personal space, as though your bodies were crammed on a subway train. Eventually he goes by, and is now slowly moving up on the Toyota. He is between your car and your unknown companion ahead, though he stays in the outside lane. You are a triangle gliding along the highway.

Then two motorcycles are behind you. They come up fast and almost right away they're on your tail. They swing out from behind your car into the passing lane, first one, then the other. The music on your radio changes when they do this, as though it knows, it feels their presence. Joe Cocker begins to sing, *give me a ticket for an aeroplane…* The motorcycles are already behind the third car, but still the driver doesn't increase his speed or change lanes. He ignores them, though they don't wait long. One motorcycle slides into the right lane, very close in front of you, and then the other follows. They move forward, slip into the passing lane in front of the third car, one, two, and they're gone. You can hear their engines fading as they speed away. The riders must be doing 160, 170. They're gone.

○

Here they are two years earlier, sitting up in a rumpled bed on a weekday afternoon. One of them is a woman, and it is unusual for her to have left the office so early. She is purposeful and collected in her work, yet still she called—*What are you doing?*—and they met here a little while ago. They drank wine and they made love with a remarkable enthusiasm for detail, and now they are having a second glass of wine. The man puts music on, music without singers. They talk, they touch each other's wonderful skin, each other's sex. They both admire the beauty of her sturdy feet. He bends his knees to bring his feet up close too, but his are thin and long, winter-white. The man's name is Tomas. Lately, he tells her, he's begun having house dreams. They aren't even living together yet. The woman says that in psychology a house is a symbol of the self.

"Did you know that? The house is a symbol of a person's own life."

The woman's name is Marie Lextase.

"You're always in the house with me."

Neither of them speaks then for what seems like a long time, absorbed in their own thoughts. She is a young married woman sitting naked in Tomas's bed in the late afternoon, leaning back on a pillow against the wall, a blanket over her legs, drinking wine from a water glass. The man is a photographer, and the walls around them are covered with photographs. More and more in the last few months there have been many pictures of her among them, a graphic display of the way she is filling his dreams. This room is their bold and secret place; the pleasure of their skin and the cold wood floor. It's a palace for them, a storybook kingdom. Harry Zeus's Pancake Heaven, he calls it, *and I am your short-order cook.* It's winter, and already growing dark outside. Her clothes are on a chair, her coat on a hook near the door.

Finally, she does ask. "Tell me about the house."

"It's empty, but we're excited because we've rented it and we're going to move in. We're thrilled. The house is very big, many of the rooms are big, but it's old and it needs to be painted, and we talk about how much furniture we'll need. It changes every time. In one dream you wished that there was a bigger balcony and then, just like that, there are two big balconies, one at the front and one at the back, and you set up a garden with a lot of clay pots. Is that my life? Are you setting up a garden of pots in my life? Maybe I'm dreaming about marijuana?"

"No." Marie smiles, but it's a worried smile too. "No. I know what you're dreaming about."

○

"The first time I was arrested was in Halifax in 1968."

This is Tomas speaking. Tomas Heyerdahl is seventy-four years old now. His son and daughter-in-law are making up the pull-out couch so he can stay at their house for the night. Lorca has brought sheets down, a pillow and a blanket, and towels. She unfurls the sheet with a crisp snap that startles the two men. They both look up. This pleases her and she smiles around at them with an exaggerated shrug.

"I used to make beds at the Colibri Hotel."

It's past midnight, and they have to get up early, but they've had a very pleasant evening, celebrating Charlie's birthday. Tomas's eyes are half-closed, and whatever he's thinking about, it's making his head loll slightly to one side and then the other. Lorca thinks maybe he's singing to himself, but now and then he gets a nice look on his face, watching them; he is happy in their company. It's been a good night. A little loose in the limbs tonight, our Grampa Tomas. Tomas is surprising his son. All three have had a fair bit of alcohol. Tomas's son is named David Heyerdahl, and David's wife is named Lorca Casal. It's after midnight and they are making up the couch so Tomas doesn't have to go home, or so David doesn't have to drive him home, or send him home in a taxi.

"Dad." David is helping Lorca tuck in the sheets but thinking about what his father said. "You never told me that you'd been arrested." When the cake was done, once Charlie had left the table to the adults, they came around to telling their youthful police stories, most of which David had heard before. His aunt had been arrested in Washington during a Vietnam War protest. *They took us away in paddy wagons. I was lucky I had my Canadian passport!* Neither David nor Lorca have ever been arrested, but three of their relatives had been picked up for underage drinking during various police raids on bars, and they compared experiences, laughing about their fake IDs, which led to reminiscing about favourite old bars and places that no longer existed. The Seven Steps. La Bodega. His uncle was picked up for drinking in a park with friends. The police didn't arrest him, but they did drive him home to have a serious conversation with his parents, which was mortifying. Through all those stories, Tomas never said a word, but now that everyone else has left, and he's half asleep in the armchair, his veiny hands folded in his lap, it seems to be his turn to talk about the past. David and Lorca are listening. David rolls his eyes—*Are you hearing this?* They'll have a lot to talk about upstairs later.

"It was during the summer, 1968. Sunday afternoon. I was nineteen years old. I had a job near the docks then, a small assembly-line job breaking down containers, and I was hanging out with a few friends the rest of the time. On a Sunday, two o'clock in the afternoon, four of us were sitting on the grass in Wellington Park, downtown. It's a square with a few benches along the paths, and a rotunda in the middle. No swings or a slide, no playground. So we were sitting on the grass, it was about two o'clock, a Sunday afternoon in July, and a police cruiser drove slowly around the park twice, looking at us. We ignored them. They stopped their car and stared at us. We ignored them. The cop in the passenger seat called out to us to move, but we acted like we didn't know they were there. Finally, they got out of the car. One of my friends stood up and left right away. Maybe we all should have done that, but we didn't. The cops came over. *What are you doing?* We said we were sitting in the park on Sunday afternoon. We smiled. We were pleasant. They took us in the car down to the police station. They put us in a pretty large room with benches and counters along each wall and left us there. It wasn't a cell, I guess it was a sort of holding room. They said they were charging us with vagrancy. *How can I be a vagrant*, I asked, *I work full time on the docks and I'm just relaxing in the park on my day off*, I said, *Leave me alone. I'm a citizen. I pay taxes.*

"The trouble was that all three of us had LSD in our pockets. We each had a tab of acid, one tab, and we had to decide what to do with it. We figured that eventually they would search us. We looked around the room for places to hide the pills to pick up later, or we talked about crushing them under our shoes.

"In the end," Tomas says, his eyes closed, waving his hand a little, "who wants to waste good acid? We took it. And we sat in the room, getting high and laughing. Maybe that lasted for an hour or two. We were able to focus and talk with the cops, as long as we didn't look at each other, and after a while they gave us papers to sign and let us go. We had to be at the courthouse about two months later. They never searched us, and we left. We went somewhere to eat."

David is both amused and surprised. He and Lorca are standing at opposite ends of the couch and she holds out her hand toward Tomas, smiling at her husband. "You did notice that he said that was the first time he was arrested?"

Tomas asks them if they take drugs, and they wait a moment before saying yes, they do sometimes smoke a joint, nothing else. "Pot and alcohol, Dad. Wine. Beer. Good single malt Scotch."

"And caffeine. My fair share of caffeine."

"Oh, I never liked pot or hash," Tomas says. "That depressed me. It felt like I was pulling a heavy blanket over my head. But I did enjoy chemicals. LSD, mescaline, cocaine."

He stands up, undoing the buttons on his shirt. "Good night, you guys. Thank you for letting me sleep here."

"Dad, you've been arrested! You have a police record!"

"Yes. A couple of times."

"Was my mother ever arrested?"

"No." He finds that an odd thing to imagine. He's smiling, already going quiet. He has decided he's not going to say any more.

Heading upstairs, Lorca puts the palm of her hand on David's back. She has been enjoying this late, weird mix of humour and discomfort. She likes Tomas. "It's not that funny," David whispers. "He's my father. Has your mother ever been arrested?"

"No, not as far as I know." She turns back. "Good night, Tomas," she calls out softly. "Sweet dreams."

"Thank you." And Tomas calls her dear: "Thank you dear. See you in the morning." Tomas lies down, but he's not relaxed anymore. He already regrets telling that story, thinking, *I should know to just shut up*. Thinking, s-w-e-e-t d-r-e-a-m-s, and he spells to himself again, s-w-e-e-t d-r-e-a-m-s, which is just something he does now with his nervous energy, n-e-r-v-o-u-s e-n-e-r-g-y.

Upstairs, Lorca and David are side by side in their own bed, hands and shoulders in the shadows of the light coming through the window. "There's a lot I don't know about my parents," David says. Lorca holds his hand up in the air over them, arms straight. When Lorca asks if he's sure he'd like to know more, David says, "Yes," but he whispers it, as though apologetically. "What about your parents?'

"Ha," she says. "My parents met briefly, though I have to say not nearly brief enough." Actually she remembers her father quite well. "I don't need to know more."

Their son turned twelve years old today. He is sleeping in the other room. They have been together for fourteen years. David's father is asleep in the living room. They have a house, a car, furniture, three bicycles, insurance, bank accounts. They have never been arrested. They are middle-class people who shop for gifts at pop-up craft fairs. They like jars of artisan chutneys, mustards, woolen scarves. These are Lorca's fortress walls. There is a bureaucratic surface to David's life, in his work and in his interaction with the world around him, including his family, but there is another part of him too, that Lorca knows, and which she saw more of in their early years together—the two of them lying in bed like this after midnight, before and after Charlie was born. This is the part that she likes to draw out, the pleasure of his company. They are lying side by side on their backs. She holds his hand straight up in the air, their arms together in the faint light from the window. She brings his hand down to her body and turns toward him.

In an Expeditionary Climate

From the air, motorcycles do make a person think of bugs.

They were moving very fast along a line that seemed watery in the summer heat, one behind the other, at times more or less close together in a kind of wing formation, the follower behind and slightly to the left or right of the leader. The bikes breezed by single cars like blips on a screen. They slipped through clusters smoothly, barely slowing down, patterned and intricate with intention.

Just east of New Benin, Ontario, the pilot of a Cessna clocked them on radar at just under 160 kilometres per hour. He spoke into a radio, and about thirty seconds later a police cruiser came out from behind an overpass, siren blaring and lights flashing. The cop in the cruiser had the pedal to the floor, chasing them, both hands on the wheel. The motorcyclists pulled over to the shoulder and turned their engines off. The cruiser came to the side of the road a few car lengths behind. The cop sat in the car for a moment watching them get off their bikes. He called in their plate numbers and waited, making some notes.

He watched them stand up, stretching, waving their arms high in the air, shaking one leg out and then the other, acting like their knees wouldn't straighten, like it was hard to walk. They seemed to be laughing at themselves. When they took off their helmets he could see that one of them was a woman, which changed things for him. It got more interesting, and the cop relaxed a little bit too. She turned toward him and he could see the outline of her hips. She was wearing a jacket with two white bands on the left arm. There was an emblem on her back. Both of the riders were smaller than the cop. He judged the man's height to be a couple of inches under six feet, and the woman was a little shorter than that. She had thick dark hair to her shoulders and her face was narrow but with pronounced features, wide cheekbones. The man had long blond hair and green eyes, a thin beard. *They don't seem much like bikers, these two*. He put on his hat, opened the door and came forward. He was a big man and he moved in a bulky way.

"Licence and registration please."

"Yes sir." The man—Tomas—answered first. "Sorry." He spoke quietly, trying to be friendly, thinking maybe he could talk his way around the tickets without being too obvious. "We have a long way to go and I guess we let that get to us." They stood in a loose circle on the side of the road. There was a wheat field behind them.

The cop appreciated their demeanour. There wouldn't be any problems. The riders were calm, smiling. He watched the woman comb her fingers through her hair. She had brown eyes, olive skin. She had a nice, open smile.

"Where are you two going?"

"We're driving across the country," Tomas said. "We're going to British Columbia. Vancouver."

Now the cop was more interested. "You're going all the way to BC on motorcycles, over the mountains? Have you ever done that before? "

It was Marie who answered him this time, with a sort of guffaw. "I don't know that we would be doing this if we'd already done it before. You'll have to let us get back to you later on that one." She spoke English with a French accent, and the cop liked the sound of her voice. Tomas has seen it happen—a person could be charmed by Marie's voice and even stay around to hear more. A voice like hers can be tempting without meaning to at all.

"How long do you expect it will take you?"

"A week and a half," she said. "It could be done in about seven, maybe eight days, if you really boot it." She held up her hand as though to say *wait, wait*. "I know," she said. "That's the reason you stopped us. We're adding three days for entertainment and two more for contingency. We're giving ourselves two weeks, but even with that we'll still be early."

This was the first day of their trip and it was a beautiful summer day. The sun was warm, the riders had that speedy adrenaline rush, and they were happy. The ticket was just a minor annoyance. They were standing on the side of the highway with the OPP officer, the three of them close to each other now. Ribbons of heat shimmered around them as they stood on the gravel at the side of the highway between the cop's car and the motorcycles.

They were discussing motorcycles now. Drivers passing by changed to the outside lane, and looked over to see, watching the threesome in their rearview mirrors. The Cessna pilot watched from above, how the three of them moved. The riders seemed looser in their bones, their shoulders. The cop could see that too. It was easy for them to shrug, and the shrug was quite expressive, it had several elements, several parts to it. He laughed to himself. They were both rather feline in that way, while the policeman, who was much bigger, was more like a dog. His name was John Bull. Maybe it's a graph scale of gender, male to female. He leaned forward, looking into the engines. "These are nice bikes." He pronounced his sentences in a way that clipped each word. He moved like that too, his shrug had only two parts, and his voice was louder and heavier than theirs, though it also conveyed a real curiosity, and there was kindness in his eyes. They could feel he was enjoying talking with them. Actually, he felt envious. They were the adventurers and he was the one slowing them down. These were no-name motorcycles, neither had any words or insignias. The only symbol was on the red bike, which had a small fish painted on the gas tank. He pointed to the woman's bike. "BMW, right?" He knew the opposed-twin cylinders. She was riding a dark grey bike, with some black and a little chrome on the engine and the pipes. It looked older but it was clean and well cared for.

Tomas pointed to the other bike. "This is a rebuilt Ducati," he said. The cop imagined an insect in the way the fender reached over the back wheel, it looked like a fly's wing, red, and with more chrome than the BMW.

"When I was a kid I had a motorcycle," the cop said. "Though really it was only a dirt bike but nobody told me that. I just rode it around the suburbs like all the other guys, though I had to reset the timing every Saturday morning. It was the wrong bike for me, but I learned a bit about engines."

"This is a touring bike," Marie said. "It's made for highways. It loves the highway, like a big dog that wants to run all day." The cop felt that she too was enjoying the conversation.

"I can see that you take good care of these bikes." He leaned over the Ducati, looking into the engine. "This looks brand new."

"Thank you. It's ten years old, but it was completely rebuilt."

"You were clocked on the radar at 158. That's very fast." He stood up, not looking at either of them, looking at the lines of the Ducati. The tank was V-shaped, and it made him think of a man's chest. A map was taped near the gas cap on the tank. "Anyway, that's too fast," he said. "The tickets are expensive."

"Both of us?" Tomas stepped back a little, giving the cop space, staying polite. "I mean, we're travelling together." He turned toward Marie. "I was in the lead and she was keeping up. If we were in a car you'd give me a ticket but not her. Not everybody inside a car gets the ticket, just the driver. It's the same as if I was the driver and she was my passenger."

The cop smiled. "That's good. I haven't heard that one

before. You were both driving motorcycles at 158 km. She could have held you back."

"How do you hold back someone on a motorcycle?"

"How do you feel about backseat drivers?"

The cop was all right. He shook his head, and turned back to his car, waving their licences in the air. "This will just take a minute."

When he returned, he left his hat on the seat of the cruiser. He gave them their papers and handed Tomas a ticket for $486. "That's four demerit points too." The cop looked at Marie. "Slow down, you two." He had turned to her to say this because of course the female is more thoughtful than the male. "You're never going to make it all the way to Vancouver like that. A rock on the road could kill you, or a shred of tire. Somebody's going to be scraping you up off the road. And then he's going to have to go home and sit down to dinner with his family. There will be a little wooden cross in the grass. Do you know about that?"

They nodded. "Yes, we know. Thank you. We'll be more careful." Tomas held out his hand and they shook. The cop couldn't remember ever shaking hands with a speeder. He turned to Marie again. He shook her small hand and then he walked back to his car.

"Have a good trip."

They climbed onto their motorcycles, helmets in their hands. "He's right, you know. Anyway," she glanced back toward the cop, "a few more of those and we'll run out of points before we even get there."

"Yes. We'll be riding around on a Greyhound."

The cop waited until they pulled out. Marie went first, which made the cop smile; he appreciated the gesture, though it probably didn't change anything. She raised one hand in a small wave back toward him. No one ever taught him how to describe the sound of a person's voice, and he would only ever have heard her voice once. She had an accent, which he liked, but her voice sounded full, the way a bell would sound, a bell with thick sides. The cop still hadn't figured out the emblem on her jacket. He couldn't go after her now, just to see, but he should have looked more closely while they were all standing around. Or maybe he should, just ride along with them for a little while. How weird would that be?

I Know What You're Dreaming Of

In the morning, Lorca is the first one downstairs. She checks on Tomas, who is sleeping, curled in an L-shape that can't be comfortable, with his head stuffed into a corner of the couch—an odd dreamer's posture. She moves quietly into the kitchen and puts on water for coffee. She can smell the neighbour outside smoking a cigarette on his deck, clearing his throat. It's 6:15 in the morning. *Yuck.* Today is Monday. She is preparing Charlie's lunch and hers when Tomas comes into the kitchen. He runs through his hair with his fingers. His shirt is buttoned but not tucked in and his feet are bare. She can see his web of veins, his toes. "Good morning, Tomas. I'm sorry if I woke you up."

"No, I always get up early." Tomas rubs the back of his neck and makes a show of breathing in the smell of coffee brewing. "That's nice to wake up to." The sun is already filtering in the kitchen windows. Lorca pours him a cup, and soon Charlie comes down to the kitchen, then David, already showered and ready to go. He kisses Lorca's neck,

he's checking email on his phone, and they sit for breakfast. Tomas sits at the far end of the table, staying out of
their morning hustle. No one is especially talkative. On
the wall in the dining room there is a large framed poster of a painting by Chagall, a young newlywed couple
floating in the air in Paris, *Les mariés de la Tour Eiffel*. The
bride is so young, her face is small and almost featureless,
a pure, baby-faced girl with waiting in her eyes, and the
groom is whispering into the girl's ear. He is touching
her hand. He is whispering that he knows he is her servant. S-e-r-v-a-n-t. *I am your servant*, the boy says. He is
her knight. Or maybe he's whispering, *Baby, let's get out of
here*, or, *I can't find my keys*. It's their wedding day, and it's
traditional to have your picture taken at the tower. The
Eiffel Tower is behind them and a goat is floating in the
air, a man is playing on a double bass or maybe it's a very
large guitar, there's a violin player turned sideways. The
chuppah is small and to the left behind them, far away, already in the past. They are floating on the back of a Chagall bird, which is unlike any other bird, and there is an
angel floating in a cloud upside down under the bird. This
is a painting of a girl in a long white dress, who looks like
someone being whispered to, and there is a boy in a dark
maroon suit, in profile, leaning close to her, saying something no one else can hear. She is holding a blue fan in her
left hand. The city is small, merely insinuated, maybe it's
just a small town outside Paris, a suburb, a few suburban
houses in 1928, to the bottom right of the painting. They
are a suburban couple. It is easy for Tomas to see them
as David and Lorca. It's an allegory. This is a painting in

the spirit of bright mornings, best with the sun coming in the window and the intimacy of a young family sitting below, planning their day. The grandfather sitting with them.

They decide that Tomas will head out with Lorca and Charlie, and she will drive him downtown after they drop Charlie off at school. Tomas would appreciate that. "I'd like to hang around downtown for a while." He winks at Charlie. "I'll get to ride in the bee-mobile." The whole family smiles, they know all the jokes about the car, her *bzz*ness. Lorca is a beekeeper. She is part of a collective that produces honey in the middle of the city, and she drives a Fiat 500 that is painted yellow with black trim, though thankfully not in stripes, with their logo on the side, an outline of a bee on the door with the words *Oasis urbaine*. Through the summer, the collective maintains colonies on the rooftops of buildings scattered around town, and they sell jars through stores and online or at weekend fairs. The workers are paid but the collective's financial viability is marginal and comes more from grants than from the little jars of honey they sell: grants in sustainability research, because bees are endangered, especially in the city, and grants for the study and development of small social enterprise. Who knew the life of a beekeeper was filled with paperwork, reports, and meetings?

From the car, Lorca and Tomas watch Charlie walk into school with a group of other students, and they sit in the car for another minute or so. "I just wait for a moment," she explains. "He's been skipping classes lately, so I like to drive him to school when I can to make sure he gets here, especially on Mondays."

"What does he do when he skips school? Does he stay home? Is he with other kids?"

"No. He's by himself. He says he likes to walk around the city. He's a people-watcher. Charlie's a twelve-year-old old man."

"He's a flaneur. That's a very honourable activity."

"Well, a couple of weeks ago he ate his lunch in the train station, and then he hung around the station for the rest of the afternoon watching the travellers. He skipped again the week after that and took a bus to the airport to spend the whole day watching people at the airport. He made a map of the airport terminals, where everything is, with stick-people in waiting lines. He says he learns more than he learns at school. He's a little smart-ass. He says people who travel spend a lot of time standing around. That's what he's learned. He watches people stand around."

"He needs a camera," Tomas says. "I'll buy him a good camera."

"Well, I'm sure he'd like that, but please don't encourage him to skip school. On top of everything else, I worry about the creepy people he's going to run into."

While they're sitting in the little car, low to the road, Lorca speaks to a colleague on her cellphone, and they arrange to meet at the warehouse later in the day. "I'm just driving my father-in-law downtown," she says, and Tomas perks up, he likes to hear her call him that.

She drops him off on Sainte-Catherine Street near Metcalfe. Tomas gets out of the car. "I'd like to go with you one day to see the beehives," he says, and Lorca nods sure, but she does not invite him along that morning.

"I'll call you soon," she says. "I'll have to bring an extra veil and gloves for you to wear."

Twenty minutes later, she is alone on the roof of a nine-story building facing Place d'Youville. Here, she can relate to Charlie skipping school, wanting to go off by himself. The morning is clear and in this part of the city a nine-story building is still high enough to see far across the river, all the way to Mont Saint-Bruno and Mont Saint-Hilaire, on the far shore. She can probably see all the way to the United States. There are seven gardens within a few blocks of Place d'Youville, small parks, a wide field behind the old stables, a lot of green. All of it is the bees' turf: parks, rooftop gardens, flowers on balconies, a florist's shop. The bees can cover five or six kilometres to bring home nectar. They are hard-working creatures and we should stand aside for them if we're in the way. Being alone with the bees is a slow, slightly meditative process, and the bees are often the best part of her day. You step into their world. Lorca is wearing a white top, her arms, neck and shoulders are bare, blue jeans, plain white Adidas. She has a small smoker she waves near the hive. The smoke quiets the bees and they pull themselves in to protect the queen, but still Lorca puts on the jacket and pulls the hood over her head. Everything is well ventilated but it's uncomfortable, hot. She pulls on gloves. It is important to be calm so the bees will stay calm, so the bees won't mind that she's there, rooting around their hive, and there are days when she can do that. She can slide out the trays to look them over one by one and the bees continue their work, accepting her presence. Bees are the most orderly community in the world, which is the only way they want it to be, but bad days are something else again. Panic in the honeycomb, which is how it will be when Tomas, a new person, is there with her.

Lorca Casal's mother grew up a in a northern suburb of Barcelona, Horta-Guinardó. Elena Casal emigrated to Canada in the early 1970s. She came here alone to work as an au pair, an adventurous young woman with a suitcase who ended up a single mother living in a small top-floor apartment in the Laurentians about a hundred kilometres north of Montreal, in a town called Sainte-Agathe-des-Monts. Charlie should chart the paths of emigrants, maybe he could explain how it is that a Spanish Jew, born in Barcelona, finds herself a grown woman living with a little girl in a snowy mountain town in Canada. Lorca grew up a country girl, and the only Spanish girl in her school, with her mother's dark eyes and her own teen-age heartbeat. She was a skier so lithe that gravity could barely hold her to the ground. Elena raised her daughter alone (the father turned out to be such a mean-spirited piece of shit it's a wonder that her mother ever willingly told him where they lived). As a teenager, Lorca worked part-time as a housekeeper at the Colibri, learning to snap bedsheets. A year or so after she was ready to leave home, moving an hour south to attend university in Montreal, her mother returned home to Spain.

In his work, David makes a point of asking himself from time to time, what is being neglected here? It might be worthwhile to ask the question of Lorca's life: what is being neglected? She and David wake in the morning to an alarm on his phone. Still sleep-soft in the skin, it takes a minute for her body to pull itself together, muscles getting into position for the dayshift. It would be so easy to return to sleep, but she's not unhappy. She stretches in bed. David's arm reaches across her shoulder and they curl together for a moment, the everyday life of spoons. How are you. She gets dressed and goes downstairs. When she was a teenager Lorca learned to be flippant—the pleasures of irony—but later she decided not to do that anymore.

There's a lot to do in the morning, but it's all easy. It's all been done before. David wakes Charlie, which is usually the most difficult task. This morning, Lorca looks in on Tomas, her husband's father, sleeping on the couch. It was not expected that he'd sleep over, but he is welcome. Lorca is quite fond of Tomas. She knows that she could depend on him, were she ever to need to, though there's no reason that she would. They leave the house and the car is almost out of gas, which is not unusual. She'll stop later. The weeks that Lorca has the car, it's always running on fumes. When she fills it she puts in twenty dollars, fifteen dollars. More than once she's had to pull over to the curb, out of gas. This is one of a number of small, everyday things that Lorca has a tendency to neglect. It's marginal for her, can't get her attention.

Who is Lorca with bees in the palms of her hands on the roof of a building on Place d'Youville? Is she the same woman she was when her hands were putting together lunches this morning, or briefly kissing her husband goodbye, *bisou, bisou, see you tonight*? David was wearing a white shirt and a striped blue tie for what he called an only semi-useful meeting that afternoon. They leaned together, he touched her lower back. He called her honey, and smiled. They talk in their own code, intertwined, their language is full of shortcuts, the marriage braid. Is she the same person when she's trying to find a place to park around Place d'Youville, frustrated, thinking *shit*? A few bees are exploring her fingers, they walk on and off her hands. Her gloves are a matte yellow and the bees are brighter, with brown bands, their wings are translucent, shiny as slivers of glass in the sun. A bee's body has no arteries, though it does have a heart and it does have a pulse. All the bee's organs float in an open circulatory system—they are goo—and the heart beats to move the blood from back to front, from the abdomen to the head, bathing all the organs and muscle tissue along the way. A bee in flight beats its wings about two hundred times every second, twelve thousand times a minute. But what is the pulse of the bee walking in Lorca's hand? What is the pulse of the unperturbed bee? What is the pulse of the unperturbed Lorca, of Lorca not running on empty? Lorca alone with the bees. She sits on a box near the hive in the sunlight. For a few minutes, she neglects everything. It may be this self who is then set aside, busy and neglected, for the rest of the day, but it's only nine in the morning; it's still early to say. This person looks into the distance, she looks down at the lush treetops in the little parks with green wire fencing and faded red metal swings, children's slides and sandboxes. She looks at the flowers

on balconies, roofs, window sills. On one balcony a squir-
rel has eaten the heads off a number of tulips, but so far
left the other plants. On another, a cat lies curled among
the flowerpots. For a moment Charlie crosses her mind,
then David, skipping like a stone on water, Tomas, dinner, the bees and their gardens, though there are also several minutes when nothing specific crosses her mind. She
enjoys the sun on her skin, the bees nearby. A small plane
passes in the distance, toward downtown. She can hear
cars below. She feels like an antenna, a receptor. Who is
she then, and how does she get from there to the woman
in the bee-mobile, thinking, half out loud, *shit, where the
hell am I going to park?*

○

The Belgian poet and playwright Maurice Maeterlinck
won the Nobel Prize for Literature in 1911, but more
importantly, he was an enthusiastic beekeeper. In 1901,
among his poems and dramatic works, he published an excellent book called *The Life of the Bee*, which was his most
popular work, and is still read today. "No living creature," Maeterlinck wrote, "not even man, has achieved in
the center of his sphere, what the bee has achieved." He
studied the mathematics of bees' architecture, their community ("the most orderly society on earth"), the division
of labour, and even their presence and contribution to the
planet.

Bisou, bisou. Lorca is David's honeybee, *my sweet honey.*
Even Charlie will say it once in a while when he's feeling

funny, *Mum, honey*. She is inured to it, a tired joke. But there are nights with David when the lights are low and their old language comes alive for them, and their kisses are as sweet as honey. Maeterlinck wondered how the bees renounced "the carnal delights of honey and love." He admired the bees' dedication and self-sacrifice.

He also wrote, "if the bee disappeared off the face of the earth, man would only have four years left to live." Now, of course, a little over a hundred years later, we'll see.

Human Figures in Motion

In the middle of a Thursday night in May, in the early 1970s, Tomas Heyerdahl, then a young man, walked across the Jacques-Cartier bridge into the city of Montreal. He had come from Halifax, Nova Scotia, about twelve hundred kilometres away, people calling out to him all along the way, *When you get tired of walking, try running, haw haw haw*. What he owned he carried in a bag on his back, and he had a knife in his pocket. He wore brown work boots and thick, dirty socks. The wind over the Saint Lawrence river was cold and the bridge shook with the weight of the trucks passing by, but the city looked like a whole display of jewels in the night, showing off for him, the lights of downtown buildings in the distance with the mild silhouette of Mount Royal behind them. Saint Helen's Island was on his right, just over the railing, with the amusement park rides, a Ferris wheel, the roller coaster scaffolding, all as though to thrill him with what might be. He stood on the bridge for a long time, just looking. Tomas's intention had been to travel to Toronto, mostly walking, unfortunately—six hundred kilometres farther—but when he stood on that bridge and looked at what felt like the most promising welcome of the city at the end of the bridge in the cool dark air, he knew he wasn't going anywhere. This was it. In the future, when he heard those old songs and stories about city gates, *Twelve Gates to the City*, *The Four-Gated City*, this image, this moment on the bridge is what he thought of. This was also how Tomas became a photographer. He kept returning to the bridge over the next few years, hoping to convey or recreate the way he felt that first night, the way he could come to feel about the world around him. He was acquiring his own lucky mythology; he understood the word epiphany.

Tomas was born at the edge of Anglo Tignish, near the northern tip on the Atlantic side of Prince Edward Island. People there have the ocean on their skin, in their pores, they hardly even notice it. They hear it in their beds at night. Tomas's mother, Nelle Brandt, died of cancer when he was seven years old. His father, Karl Heyerdahl, was a fisherman. Tomas was their only child and after his mother died he grew up mainly on his own, sort of feral or maybe just an introvert, unsophisticated, withdrawn, lonely. He missed as much school as he attended (which made it easy for him to understand his grandson now), wandering across the fields and building forts out of stone and branches—places to hide, to be alone, reading books from the church basement sale. His father was away every day at sea or else in some bar, often all the way in Charlottetown. At fifteen, Tomas left school and joined his father on the boat. He fit in well, but he was only fifteen years old, and what kind of life was that? He didn't mind the hardship. *If you want to know what prayer is, turn toward the sea.* He did a man's work, and he laughed at men's jokes, but at seventeen he left. He moved away without giving it much thought, took a bus to Charlottetown and soon was living in a rooming house in the neighbourhood near the university, glad to be on the street around people his own age, and especially glad to be among so many girls. He made friends. He was quiet, attentive, willing. It was a new way of living for him, and he soaked it in. His friends were students and they accepted him as one of their own, though he was an outsider. Compared to them he was uneducated but he was untethered, freer than they felt themselves to be. School did not ground him. For a while, nothing did. Tomas became a petty thief, a shoplifter, an occasional drug dealer. Through the winter months he'd run into his father now and then in bars. Sometimes he turned away, sometimes they shared a drink or money. Eventually Tomas migrated from Charlottetown to Halifax, where he spent two more years in a kind of limbo, waiting, working in a warehouse, living in a room, spending his nights in bars. He could not have said what he was waiting for; this was a time to find change in himself. It was his own silence that brought him through those years, the reticence of a motherless child. He was often content to withdraw to his room and read.

That same spring, the woman who would become David's mother, Marie Lextase, was living with her parents in Cartierville, on the last block of Jasmin Street, which ended in a cul-de-sac on the banks of the Rivière des Prairies, one of those little cubby-hole corners of the city: stone or brick homes with the river just down the block and a lot of tall, old trees reaching out over the street and giving it a haunted air. It was a scary place to walk alone on a dark winter night. On the next block was Beausejour Park with a fence along the river, a duck pond, and a monument to veterans of the two World Wars. Marie's father was named Albert Lextase, and he had been taught since he was a child to be precise. You could hear it in the way he spoke. He was born in Montreal a year after his family came to Canada from Algeria. Albert had two older sisters. The children became North American, secular. Albert served as a nurse near the end of WWII, was accepted into medicine at the Université de Montréal, and went on to become a cardiac surgeon at Sacré Coeur Hospital on Gouin Boulevard. Albert was a tall stick of a man, with good hands and the right inquisitive temperament for such intricate work, fine and messy. Albert married a charming Québécoise, Madeleine Tardif, who was an administrator in public education. They had one child—their brilliant daughter. While Tomas was walking out of Halifax, Nova Scotia, Marie was finishing her last year at the École polytechnique, the Université de Montréal's school of engineering. Women engineering students were still quite rare in those years, and Marie was one of only two in her graduating class.

Another spring, as the snow was melting, Tomas took more than a hundred photographs of bicycles that had been left outside through the winter, left forgotten, chained to fences and poles. Bicycles that had rusted, their wheels crushed by snow plows, the frames bent, pieces missing, wheels, seats, gears, brakes—sometimes all of it was stripped and gone, nothing but the frame lying across the sidewalk chained to a pole, people stepping around it. The Blanc Gallery exhibited a show of his bicycle pictures, forty-two photos, and the show received some attention around the city. Walking through the exhibit left people with a sense of negligence and loss. The annual urban ritual was a show of preposterous material waste, a comment on our disposable culture. The show was reviewed twice, and Tomas sold some pictures. The gallery sold a small print of one of the pictures, and a young painter named Timothée Villiers gave Marie Lextase a copy with her birthday present (a sweater). She put the print on her refrigerator door. At the time Marie and Tim were talking about marriage. She was also studying machinery, including beautiful motorcycles.

In May, 1972, all of Quebec's trade unions joined in a general strike, a common front across the province that lasted for a month. It was the largest strike in North American history. Workers took over radio stations and government buildings in nine cities. Tomas jumped in. He was with the demonstrators every day, every night, taking photographs. He took a bus up to Saint-Jerome, wanting to follow the strike in a smaller city, to be closer to the demonstrators, but it was too hard to get around without a car. He was soon begging rides back and forth every morning and night, or staying over, sleeping on cots. He headed farther to Mont Laurier, and then all the way to Cabano, five hundred kilometres north of Montreal.

In these small cities and towns, the strike took over everyone's lives in a way that was less absorbing in Montreal. He slept on people's couches, he met their children, he helped put out the garbage; he photographed assemblies. It was in Saint-Jerome that Tomas was arrested for the second time in his life, with a group of strikers who were pulled in one night for disturbing the peace and loaded into a yellow school bus. As a photographer he was an outsider, and the police were ready to leave him alone, but he wanted to be with the others and it wasn't difficult to provoke the cops into taking him too. He wanted some pictures of the strikers sitting together on the bus, to photograph their emotions, their anger and worry, he wanted to hear them talk. He even got a few pictures in the police station, before the cops put away his camera, which they did carefully. Tomas sold photographs to news agencies or sometimes straight to the newspapers themselves, or magazines, and this is how he became a professional photographer—first a stringer, and eventually, later, an employee. While Tomas was still freelancing, he began shooting weddings and family portraits on the side.

The spring after that, Marie Lextase was employed by Bombardier Transportation Americas, an engineer in a company of engineers. They were working on a project to deliver 368 subway cars to the city of Philadelphia. Marie was working long days cluttered with meetings, and she was planning her wedding to Timothée that July. They would be married in an orchard on a bright summer day. They would dance to *Signed, Sealed, and Delivered*.

She would leave her parents' house and come into another way to live; they would begin another part of their lives together. Tomas was walking across the city again, this time taking photographs of empty stores with for-rent signs in the windows. Again, he created a series of forty-eight photographs giving a pervasive feeling of the city as a wasteland. Unwanted. Dust and cobwebs: you could see that every shop had been empty for a long time. The kraft paper or newspaper that had been taped up to line the windows was tearing, turning grey or yellow. The windows themselves were filthy and painted over with graffiti, and the for-rent signs were hanging crooked or had fallen to the floor. The Blanc Gallery held a show the following autumn and he took it as a happy, minor achievement. Those people who saw both exhibits remarked on their similarity in subject and sensibility. Tomas was reviewed in a weekly paper as "a poet of abandonment and waste." For some people there seems to be only one concern that they're really compelled to express, and they do it over and over, more or less developed or more or less disguised as something different. They could be defined by their preoccupation, and it might have been an interesting question for the reviewer to ask him, *Do you choose this or not? Do you ever feel you got it right?* Tomas was invited to parties, making his way into the city's art crowd. How many people knew of him now? Fifty people, two hundred? One night, during the vernissage at the Blanc Gallery, with his storefront pictures on the wall, Tomas was introduced to Marie and Timothée. Timothée was already one of Canada's important young painters, *Top*

Thirty Under Thirty, and an assistant professor at the Université du Québec à Montréal. Both Marie and Timothée liked Tomas's photographs, and Tomas said thank you. He stayed with them for a few minutes. He knew most of the people there that night as acquaintances, and he had seen Marie and Timothée in passing at one event or another. Tonight was his party and guests were coming to him to offer congratulations, *Great collection*, offering him another drink. Marie and Timothée seemed to know everyone, and their attention wavered from Tomas to others and back again. He was struck by her quick smile and the expressiveness of her gestures, her friendliness. She seemed to draw in a breath to speak when a friend came to her. *How are you?* She touched someone's arm. It was Tomas's night but they were more popular than he was; he found it impossible to hold a conversation, though he got more attention just by standing near them. They were attractive, well dressed, adult.

"I saw your review in the paper. Congratulations."

"Thank you." He said it was good to have the attention; he hoped that more people might come to see the pictures. He shook his head, "But it isn't poetry."

And that was the evening when they met, introduced themselves. Marie looked at him in that way she had when she noticed something that piqued her curiosity. In the years to come he would call it radar. He felt her watching him while Timothée talked of his own experiences with art reviews. "Even the good ones are a disappointment," he said; such a luxurious thing to say. Tomas was more interested in Marie's opinion.

The three of them stood near the wall with drinks in their hands, people moving around them. Marie was curious about what she took to be Tomas's reserve. "You're not working the room," she said, and he shrugged. It was losing importance. They talked for a few minutes longer. A friend pulled Timothée away for a moment and the gallery director came and pulled Tomas away too. For the next hour or so, he wound his way back to them twice. He watched her take a breath, enjoyed her friendliness. *How's it going?*

Of course, Timothée didn't think of photography as art. "It's too literary," he said to Marie on their way home. "It's exactly poetry. A picture is a thousand words, right?"

○

Marie has always had a preference for black notebooks with flexible covers, about the size of a regular book. She can carry them with her through the day. The pages are ruled, and sometimes in grids. Her handwriting is smooth and neat. She usually writes in blue ink. Rarely is a word or a paragraph crossed out; she composes her thoughts before she writes them down, she knows what she intends to write. She takes her time, and she writes in these books almost every day of her life. She also glues or tapes in pictures or texts from magazines or other sources, notes in other people's handwriting. There are sketches, quotations. The books are grab bags, daybooks, a thinking practice.

Tuesday, April 23, 1977. Yesterday evening, Tomas put a stool in the middle of the dining room, and cleared away everything around it. He bought a huge roll of white paper to cover the floor and the space behind the chair so there was only the white background, and he asked me to sit. The illusion was that I was sitting in an empty white space. He had bought a blue silk scarf, and he pulled my hair back and tied the cloth over my eyes. I knew he was going to do this, he'd warned me. The scarf was beautiful, shiny and long, and the ends of the blindfold hung down past my shoulders. I sat still, thinking to myself, *be Zen, om, om, oh shit, distraction, om,* blindfolded like that for a while. Maybe it was only five or ten minutes, but it seemed much longer. I think he waited so long for me to become less conscious of the scarf. We talked about other things. Work. He played music. The camera clicked a few times, but after a while began to click more often. *Here we go.* After a few minutes he asked me to stand. "Don't touch anything, just stand." He said that it would be very helpful if I could levitate, and I offered my apologies. "Touch nothing," he said. I was blind, of course. I tried not to follow the camera, not to turn my head at every click of the shutter. And then I changed my mind, and I did turn my head at every click, responding like an animal. I tried to let my face go slack and then react. I paid attention to the sounds around us and the way the air felt on my skin. The refrigerator hummed—all the noises I usually ignore. I listened to Tomas moving, and to the click of his camera. I tried to imagine what he was looking at, what he saw. Sometimes I am flattered by the camera, and there are days when I quite enjoy flattery, vain enough for that. The silk is a deep indigo colour and in the pictures it turned out quite striking against my skin and hair. At one point I did notice a faint light at the bottom of the blindfold, and I adjusted the silk to cover that spot too. No cheating. I imagine that Tomas was expecting me to be apprehensive, but there wasn't much to worry about. Tomas was taking my photograph. Tomas, who said I would be a good poker player because I didn't show much emotion unless he asked me to smile or frown. Without being able to see the eyes, it's difficult to visually capture a person's emotion—someone sitting on a chair, or standing in empty whiteness as though floating in the air. In the end, it's the viewer who will read into the photograph. Something, the colour of silk against the colour of skin will catch the viewer's attention, and the viewer will feel the emotion that Tomas intended, what he put into the photograph. For the viewer it's probably a momentary and shallow transaction, I think. Tomas asked me to walk forward a few steps, then go back. I held my hands in front of myself, but only a little. It was awkward to sit back down on the stool; I nearly fell. Tomas continued to move around the room and every once in a while the camera clicked. He asked me often how I was doing. "Would you like anything? Everything all right? We can stop anytime you wish," he said, but I could tell he was enjoying it— this was good. At the end, I felt his hands on my neck, which I liked, his fingers on my collarbone, and the camera clicked for one last time, very close to me. I felt his lips brush my neck, and I turned my head to meet him. Tomas took my hands in his and I stood up. I decided to keep the blindfold on a little while longer.

This afternoon he printed a dozen photographs of me with the silk over my eyes like that and pinned them on the cork wall. They were all head-shots only, my mouth and my hair, my nose, eyebrows. Some colour, some black and white. "What is this about?" I asked him. "Are you saying that a woman doesn't see, or that a woman can't see or a woman shouldn't see?"

No. He was surprised by the question. "It's not a general image," he told me. "It's not a social comment, it's specific to you, it's a photograph of you. I see you as vulnerable and strong at the same time." That's what he was thinking about. "Justice is blind," he said, "but justice is vulnerable." A good line, one I'm sure he was making up. "Traditionally, justice is a blindfolded woman," he went on. We both smiled. I think we were both imagining a ridiculous version of me with the scales of justice in my hand. "Anyway, most of your vulnerability is artificial. Not of your own making."

"Whose making?"

He didn't know what to say. "Mine, I guess." He shrugged. Tomas isn't used to having to explain his work, to articulate the reasons for what he does. He chose the easy way out. "The truth is that I just thought it might be a good picture," he said. "Just look."

I have grown comfortable with this role in his photography, I'm a colleague. It doesn't touch me so much anymore to see myself like that on the wall. I am a subject: there's me and there's the other on the wall. Many are not really pictures of me, but of an idea, a blindfolded woman. Still I do wonder where will this take us. Is Tomas a person who would sell photographs of his own wife? What does that mean for me? How detached am I willing to be?

You and Me and a Map

They had driven out of Montreal around nine in the morning, just after the traffic rush cleared. They had a friend, William Munk, who was also making the Vancouver trip, but on his own, leaving two days later and bringing all the framed photographs in his van. Tomas checked in with him three times that morning before he would finally walk out of the house and lock the door. "Hey, Munk, we're leaving now."

"Okay, Tomas. You can stop phoning me. Everything is fine, don't be so nervous. We've already packed the truck. I will leave on Wednesday morning. I'll see you there. I'll get there before you."

"Have a good trip, but remember to keep in touch. Any news at all, leave a message with Klara. All right?"

"Absolutely, brother, I'm looking forward to this."

They were travelling light but still the bundles tied down behind them changed the balance of the motor-cycles: clothing, a small tent, a double sleeping roll, and three cameras all strapped onto their bikes behind them, the riders leaning forward with their orb helmets. Blue and yellow. It's a great feeling to be leaving town. We humans are excellent at setting aside, compartmentalizing, and it's possible that more of the person we really are comes forward when we are leaving, unencumbered by commitments and expectations, relations with other people. *Salut, là.* They were leaving for a month, and within a few blocks life was already simpler, just the two of them, you and me and a map, travelling alone, with the mechanics of the bikes in their feet and in their hands, in their wrists, driving north on Saint-Laurent Boulevard with the first part of their trip taped onto their gas tanks.

They lived on Drolet Street, not far from Mont-Royal Boulevard, across from a little park that someone had named after a Québécoise singer, where a hand-painted plywood sign read *Parc Nanette Workman*. They had a small two-story rowhouse, with an aloe plant in the front window onto the sidewalk and wrought iron over the window. There was a skylight in their bedroom upstairs, a lane in the back that led to their yard, and a place for the bikes. There was a jar on top of the fridge where they dropped their change. Marie was an engineer and Tomas was a photographer, and this trip they were on was about photography. The trip was for him. They were travelling across the country for a showing of his work. Tomas was not a well-known photographer and the invitation had come as a surprise to him. His first show outside the province of Quebec. His first show west of Park Avenue. He wondered if it was a mistake that they chose him, but he didn't ask. In the end, it would turn out to have been his only solo exhibit outside Quebec.

There was artwork all over their walls at home, not all of it his. They each had a room for their work, a dark-room and an office. Photographs and sketches pinned to their cork boards. They shared a nice high bed. Tomas was a photographer, and Marie had become his principal subject.

One starry night in the darkness of Northern Ontario they were making love in the woods, inside their little green tent. The tent was quite small, small enough to strap onto the back of a motorcycle, and it seemed likely to fall over them at one point or another. They were trying to move without moving, to give themselves over, abandon but with the utmost constraint. It was midnight and other campers nearby could hear their laughter. You could see the outline of her knee pressing into the wall of the tent. The man in the Cessna looked down through the trees and smiled. *If the tent's a-rockin', don't come knockin'*. But inside the tent they were more serious, mindful of each other's body, pleasure. The writheless fuck. They were looking for a rhythm that wouldn't pull the tent down.

One of them snores, the other really doesn't. One of them crawls out naked in the middle of the night to piss in the trees, his porcelain skin glowing in the moonlight.

o

The foot is more beautiful than the shoe. Actually, Michel-angelo said more noble. The foot is a noble and intricate part of the organism that is the noble and intricate body.

A quarter of all the bones in our bodies are in our feet: twenty-six bones, thirty-three tiny joints. There are one hundred muscles, tendons, and ligaments in our small beautiful feet, size seven, size nine, ten, eleven. Michelangelo also said, *skin is more beautiful than the garments which clothe it*. The skin rejoices. Tolstoy, on the subject of footwear and self-deprecation, said late in his life, *A good pair of boots is worth more than* War and Peace.

In the morning, Marie and Tomas dressed. They boiled water with a little pot and a Sterno can. Sunlight finding them through the trees. Marie was sitting at a picnic table drinking green tea from a hot metal cup and writing in her diary: *It is wonderful to be travelling like this, though with a long way to go. We are in a campground in Algonquin Provincial Park, not quite to North Bay. The ghost of Tom Thomson is tramping around here. There's a recurring urge to call out to him. Tomas and I walk down to Canoe Lake from our tent. We swim in the water where Tom Thomson died. We bought postcards. I think we will stay here and put off Lake Superior for another day. Yesterday the big cop gave Tomas a speeding ticket for $486.*

They used the camp showers and packed up. Before leaving they walked through the woods that surrounded the campground. Tomas carried all three cameras rather than leave them unattended, one camera hanging around his neck, the others in a case across his shoulders. They walked through the trees and slowly separated, drifting through the forest. He took a few photos of Marie through the trees, going up a hill. They lost sight of each other but they knew they weren't far apart. Marie was looking at the ground, the gnarly roots of trees. There were vines growing along the earth and fallen trees she walked beside, climbed over, moss all around. Tomas was more interested in the way the sunlight was coming through the tops of the trees. He took a few photos of shafts of light in the branches. At the top of a hill he caught sight of Marie across a gully, about a hundred metres away. She was walking onto a small wooden bridge, coming in his direction. He called out and she looked up. He took a few pictures of her crossing the wooden bridge. He did not change the lens for a closer focus, but let the distance stand as it was, to make a photo of a woman walking on a foot bridge. He decided the photograph would have to be very large, framed on a wall, and her body would be small in those surroundings, a background of trees, over-whelmingly green. Marie's body was the focal point in the photo of the forest, the foot bridge a crooked line.

His pictures were filed in cabinet drawers. Looking is omnivorous, gluttonous; the mind in our gaze always wants more. They were pinned up on the walls. There was a drawer full of cardboard envelopes of negatives, years of negatives, numbered and named. There were cameras and accessories around the rooms of their house, left here and there, a tripod on the floor under a leather chair, on the table near the door, strips of negatives and contact sheets beside the bed. There were pictures everywhere. They had a hallway upstairs and one wall was lined with cork. He put new pictures on the cork every day and took others down.

Monday, 17 October, 1978. I don't mind being photographed so long as I am moving, but if I have to be still, that's another matter. The wait to be photographed, the posing, makes my skin crawl. I can certainly understand why people felt that the camera was stealing their souls. Look at their faces. A camera could steal my soul. And imagine, the exposures were so slow then, some had to wait for fifteen minutes. That is excruciating. People who were posing wore braces attached to the backs of their heads to keep them from moving and ruining the image. That's why no one is smiling in those photographs. It's impossible to hold a smile for fifteen minutes, it's impossible to be so still. Their whole lives must have passed before their eyes, they could feel their souls leaving their bodies, looking into the mysterious machine. They knew they would be turned into images of themselves. Photography was the devil. There is no other reasonable explanation.

o

They ate an apple and almonds and then didn't eat again until they got off the highway looking for a diner and a gas station in a little town called Elaine. They parked outside in a small lot, the motorcycles leaning side by side. They were eating in a booth by the window. On her way in Marie had picked up a tourist brochure for a place called Falcon Lake, Manitoba, where there had been a UFO sighting in 1967, and they were deciding whether they should drive there or not, to look. "It will just be a field where something once happened." Marie was pulling pieces of cucumber out of her sandwich and Tomas was watching her fingers. She wore two rings. He took the cucumber off her plate and ate it himself. Their helmets on the seats beside them.

A family, a man and a woman and a small boy, walked by them and the man nodded. "Nice bikes." They sat in a booth and the man looked up often, watching Marie while they ate lunch: a woman with a motorcycle helmet on the seat beside her. His wife watched him, pointedly, until he finally snapped at her. "What?"

Outside, Marie and Tomas zipped on their jackets, and put on their helmets and popped down the visors. The man and the woman were both watching. The bikes idling. The back of Marie's jacket had the image of a hawk in flight.

After Elaine, they worked their way through a long thread of cars. When they were almost clear, a silver Porsche R pulled into the lane behind them. The driver had decided to match their speed, or maybe he was thinking he'd race them. He was driving too close behind Marie. And now he wasn't bored, he was having fun, it was like pushing a dog in the ass with the toe of your shoe. She slid to the inside lane to let him pass, but he followed her inside, too close, he could almost touch her rear tire. She looked at him in the mirror, and he was laughing. Once they were through the thread into the open she sped up to 165, 170. She was rigid, hanging on, trying to stay calm, but still he stayed with her. The two motorcycles were pushing 180 now, and Tomas moved into the outside lane and then slowed down. Marie went by him on the inside, and then the Porsche was beside him. For a moment, Tomas turned his head toward the driver, but they were going too fast to look away from the road. For a second Tomas lifted his left hand off the grip and held it out with his palm down. The driver laughed, *fuck you*. Tomas slowed down, letting the car move ahead of him and then the car jerked into the outside lane.

As he came abreast of Marie she slowed her bike down quickly, letting him go right by, and then he was ahead of them, on his own. The two motorcycles came down to 120, 100, then 90, 80. The car disappeared. He honked his horn. The long line of traffic had caught up now, and cars began to pass them. They drove off at the next exit and pulled over on the side of the road.

"What the fuck was that?" She was furious. They got back onto the highway, but she pulled off again at the next rest stop. She drove slowly through the parking lot, up and down, looking for the silver Porsche, but it wasn't there. They went back onto the highway and drove another eighty kilometres to the next rest stop, where they pulled off again, cruising through the parking lot, but the Porsche wasn't there either. She finally parked her bike anyway. "Whatever, shit. He could have killed me." Marie has lived a life of discrete privilege—private schools, clubs, engineering at the Polytechnique. She was not a person accustomed to being pushed around for entertainment. Tomas knew more about that than she did.

He wasn't surprised at the Porsche. He and Marie sat outside with sandwiches and tea for a long time.

"That guy wasn't really thinking anything," Tomas said. "Never. Not an awareness in his head. He didn't decide to go after you, it just happened, and he'd probably say that you were never in danger. He didn't touch you. People do things and maybe think about it later. We are barely conscious, we accumulate events. Things happen like they're pebbles dropped into the pool and the water in the pool splashes."

They walked through the gift shop looking at T-shirts and maps of the roads ahead. Are you all right? Yes. Let's go.

Still, at the next rest stop, an hour later, Marie did take the lead and pull off again. They cruised slowly through the parking lot. "I'd really like to talk to that asshole." But of course he wasn't there, and they returned to the highway. The thing is, she is going to see the driver again, but it won't be for another week, just when she's grown used to the idea of what happened, when she'll have stopped thinking about it, and there he'll be with his look-at-me smirk, and she won't know what to do with him.

The Everyday Life of Spoons

Imagine that you are Lorca Casal sitting alone on the rooftop of a six-story building in the Plateau neighbourhood, just a block from Laurier Park. Say you are on a rooftop, sitting alone, close to any large park with flowers and trees and ducks in a pond in the city where you live. There are bees in the flowers that arc over the pond. It's morning, summer, you are sitting at a picnic table on the roof with your phone in your hands, flipping through a few news sites and then Facebook to see what's up, mostly friends sharing pictures of famous people posing with their wedding cakes.

You look through your bag and take out a lottery ticket that you haven't checked yet. The draw was the night before and when you pull up the lotto site and read the numbers, it turns out that the ticket in your hands is a big, big winner. An enormous winner! It is the winner! You have a ticket that appears to be worth twenty-three million dollars. A little blue piece of paper. Imagine what that moment would be like for you. How would that go?

What would happen? Your heart is pounding and all your nerves are spiked. You're on a great adventure. You read the numbers again, of course, and then you check them again. Is there a point at which you would scream? You are up on the roof of a building so a few people below might look around but no one would see you, no one would care. You are alone. You stand up; could you sit down? How many times would you read the numbers? Ten, twenty, how many more? A hundred? Would you imagine how it would be to have so much money? You read the numbers again. You read them again. Do you think about what you would buy? Is there a thing you'd most like to own? Do you think about how the money will change your life, has already changed your life from this very minute forward? This is probably something you've thought about in the past, winning so much money, and have already vaguely and with great enjoyment imagined what you would do with it if you ever won. Did you think about generously giving money to your friends and charities? Do you think about all the people who are going to ask you for money? They're going to offer you investment opportunities. Do you think that the first thing you should do is hire a lawyer? Would you call your husband or wife or someone else close to you right away, or would you wait a few minutes? How will it change their lives? Time has already passed. You have already waited a while reading over the numbers so many times, letting it sink in. You are still reading the numbers, over and over again. You look at the sky. You look at the park. Your knees are twitching, your body can't be still. You look at the roofs of other buildings nearby, but you don't think at all about what you see. You are in some other mental state, hardly recognizable, your nervous system has taken over. Do you think it would be an hour before you called someone you love? The phone is right there in your hand, and the winning ticket is in the other hand. You have come to believe that you are a winner. It's true. You accept it. Would hours pass, four hours, before you call? You may think to yourself, what should I do? Money plays such an integral role in our lives, like the air we breathe, but we still have to guard against the temptation to let it play too important a role as a measuring stick, not just of our success, which is already a questionable truth, but more importantly of who we are. We wear money sewn into our clothes, often by young people in Bangladesh, money woven into our hair, in our voices, our brittle minds, in the way we talk to people. What would you do?

Lorca walks around the roof for almost three hours with the winning ticket in her hand, a bundle of anxious energy. She worries that the sweat from the palm of her hand might erase the numbers. The bees come to her, drawn by the activity, and she has to slow herself down, but still many of the bees stay near as though they are watching her, as though they know her, their Lorca. They are accompanying her, concerned for her. She does not call David, or anyone else. A colleague texts her from the office a few times. *Where are you? I need the car this afternoon.*

She passes the rest of the day obsessing about the twenty-three million dollars in her wallet, a little blue piece of paper, and it only adds to her anxiety. She is afraid of what the money will do to her family, and the longer she waits to call David, the weirder she feels about it. She imagines him asking, *You're only calling me now?* Though really, why would that be the question he'd ask?

Lorca says out loud, to no one, to the bees, "Shit, I don't want this."

○

In his daily life, David Heyerdahl is employed by a company that specializes in water filtration. The company exists on a large, international scale: they work with the flow of rivers—the Nile, the Danube, the Ox-Bow, the Rouge. They study dams and ecosystems, contamination, and oceans, oceans as though they were ponds, and actual ponds. They study industrial waste, civilizational waste, mercury, microplastics, sheets of plastic floating into the bellies of whales, picnic coolers floating into the bellies of whales, and everything is named and measured in tonnes and macro-tonnes. And at some level outside their influence, of course, everything is denied or renamed. They work with governments, from national to municipal, and they work with corporations, designing ways the organizations can clean up after themselves, their accidental spills, their resultant spills, their intentional dumps. David's office is on the twenty-seventh floor of a tower in downtown Montreal, but the company has a number of offices around the world, and the head office is in Paris.

Today, Tomas is meeting his son for lunch. The receptionist calls David to say that Tomas is there, and Tomas waits on a chair across the room, keeping his mask on. There's been another warning and everyone is wearing their masks downtown this week, breathing away from each other, keeping some distance. Tomas leafs through a copy of *Irrigation Magazine*, pictures of water and pipes a man can walk through. In a few minutes David comes out with two tall men who stop for a moment and say thanks again. They are wearing blue masks with a small red maple leaf in the corner. As they go out the door David points to them. "RCMP," he says to Tomas.

Tomas has come thinking he might ask David about drugs today, he's been thinking about that lately, how he'd like to get some, but David is excited about the RCMP. "It's the third time they've been here," he says. An elevator stops but they step back because it's too crowded. David presses the button again. "They're investigating a guy named Robert Barton. He's a lifelong bureaucrat, a party hack from Manitoba." They get on a second elevator and ride down while David is talking, even though there's another person in the elevator, which surprises Tomas. David talks as though the person isn't even there. "He worked for one level or another of the party for thirty-two years, working to get them elected, and once the Conservatives finally did win federally, they repaid him with a senior position in Northern Affairs. A pretty nice gig, well paid."

They walk outside to a restaurant in a tower across the street. Just a couple of tables on the ground floor. "It's small," David says, "but the food is good."

They order at a counter and then choose a table by a

window. "Barton put together a phony water treatment company, and the RCMP say it's officially owned by his girlfriend"—he makes quotation marks with his fingers in the air—"now she's his 'fiancée', and over the last two years he siphoned off money by making sure that contracts were awarded to her company. They say the total is about thirty-two million dollars, but it's probably more." A server brings their lunches to them on trays, pasta for both of them, bread, bottles of water. "Dad, Robert Barton is sixty-six years old, and his girlfriend is twenty-two. Her name is Valerie Wilson and before they met she worked for an escort service in Ottawa. She was a hooker." He stops talking for a moment now, eating, putting butter on a roll. "How's your pasta? It's good, isn't it?"

"So, the RCMP have been around our office a few times lately asking about the system, how the whole system works, how the water industry works, filtration plants. The case is supposed to go to court in the next year or so, although even that isn't sure because the trial keeps being postponed for one reason or another. The biggest issue here is that the funds were intended to improve water availability for Indigenous people living in the North. They haven't had good water in thirty, forty, eighty years. The rumour now is that Barton has cancer. I think the government would be happy if he were sick and they'd be happy to postpone the whole thing until he dies. He's an embarrassment. Apparently the prosecutors are talking about charging him with lobbying, which is complete bullshit. The government wants to hide him away. They want to charge him with working as an unregistered lobbyist, which is nothing, and she won't be charged at all."

○

It's only on the way back to the office that Tomas asks David how he buys pot, trying to get it in before David has to go upstairs. "Do you have a drug dealer? Tell me about your drug dealer."

David shakes his head. "Dad, I don't know a drug dealer. I get pot or hash sometimes from my friend Ed. He buys it for me; he must know a dealer. But Lorca and I really don't smoke very often. You shouldn't imagine that."

"What's Ed like? Do you think he'd mind if you asked him to get something for me?"

"Ed's a good friend. Yes, I could ask him for some-thing. Do you want some pot, hash?" But Tomas has something else in mind. "I'd like to get some LSD." And then he says it again, before David can speak. "I'd like to get some acid," and he says it like he's savouring the word or the idea.

"Are you kidding me? What do you want with LSD?" David stops on the sidewalk. "I can't get you LSD."

"Why not? I've done it before. You don't need to worry, I'm a very rational person. I've never tried to jump off a building or eat a door or anything like that."

"Dad, this is too weird. Why do you want LSD?" Robert Barton and his girlfriend are gone from his mind.

"I just want that feeling of wonder again. I won't take

a lot, half a tab. Do they still make it in tabs? Ask him if they still make Purple Haze, or Blue Cheer. I'll only take a half dose. But tell Ed that it can't be cut with speed. Tell him it shouldn't be cut with anything. I want just pure acid." He pauses. "I wonder if I've ever had pure LSD?"

"Ed isn't a drug dealer. He's my friend. We are members of a tennis club." David says they wear whites and drink beer under an umbrella when the match is over. "We might share a joint if no one's around." Some afternoons they play doubles with their wives and have dinner at the club. The kids swim in the pool together. "I doubt that Ed knows much about speed and Blue Cheer, but maybe I'm underestimating him." David is relenting, he can feel himself giving in. "Okay, but I want to be with you when you do it," he says. "I'll be there to make sure you're all right."

Tomas nods. "That would be fun, and it might be a good idea. Drugs have probably changed since the last time I dropped acid."

"You think?" David nods. "I'll talk to Ed and ask if he can get some." Tomas has a big smile on his face. David hasn't seen that in a long, long time. When does the son see the father smile like that? "Oh, Dad."

In the evening, when they're alone, David tells Lorca about his father's request. They talk about it on the couch. She's been in an excited mood herself this evening (she just won twenty-three million dollars, though David doesn't know this); she is light, infectious. She finds a joint and they go outside to smoke it and talk about the dangers of LSD. Tomas is an old man. "I think he's bored,"

David says, "but he says he's not bored, he's just not excited either. He says he doesn't feel much of anything."

"I think he's lonely," Lorca says. "Are you going to ask Ed for him?"

"Yes, I guess I will. Who am I to chaperone my father, like now I'm the father? Who am I to tell my father how to live? But I think I should be with him. I'd like to be there to keep an eye on him when he does it."

"Will you take acid with him?"

This makes them both laugh. "Huh," he says, as though he hadn't thought of that. "I guess I will."

Marie, Muybridge, and the Ducati

Eadweard Muybridge was a photographer and inventor most famous for his work in the 1870s as part of what began as a research project for Leland Stanford, a Californian politician and tycoon. Stanford was the man who put his name on Stanford University. He was also a robber baron and one of the Big Four who built the Central Pacific Railway. Leland Stanford had a problem. He made a bet that couldn't be settled: to win he needed proof that, when a horse trotted or ran, there were moments when it raised all four hooves off the ground at the same time, when it did not touch the ground. Muybridge designed a series of multiple cameras to capture movement in a kind of stop-motion photography, a number of cameras laid out in a line and set off by the horse touching trip wires as it ran by, click, click, click, click. For the first time, people were able to see the intricacies of movement, all the details that the human eye could not see by itself. "Only photography," Muybridge wrote, "has been able to divide human life into a series of moments, each of them has the value of a complete existence." Stanford won his bet.

Marie and Tomas were at home on Drolet Street. She was slicing carrots and sliding them off the wooden board into a soup pot on the stove. They had been living here for almost a year. Their own home, their kitchen. The door to the back balcony was open but they were standing near the counter with glasses of wine, crackers and cheese. "Only a photographer would suggest that each photograph has the value of a complete existence," she told Tomas.

Tomas just smiled, slow to respond. "Well...." She waited. These were the conversations she liked, the discussions, her mind snapping ahead, one–two, the merits of an argument, but Tomas is less educated and not as adept as she is at the art of conversation. He could feel what Muybridge was getting at. "It was a hundred years ago." They discussed this for a while, leaning against the counter beside the soup cooking on the stove, but then Tomas came back to her two days later. "You can see the core of life in a gesture, the vibrancy of life even in the way a person points a finger." He put a photograph into her hands. "I can take a picture of the moment you turn to look up with something on your mind and there is purpose in the line of your jaw, in your eyes." He smiled, pointed at her photograph. "Look, what are you thinking in this picture?"

Through knowing Tomas, Marie had become more interested in photography, and curiosity drew her to learn more. On the way home sometimes she stopped at the UdeM library, leafing through monographs, randomly reading histories of photography. She experimented with pinhole cameras made out of cardboard boxes, landscape photography, things that wouldn't move because she needed crazy exposure times—eight, ten, twelve, twenty minutes. She tried different-sized boxes and different shapes. She added a mirror; glass; she bought radiographic film, 14"x17". Her negatives were pinned on the walls now too, and there were boxes wrapped in duct tape here and there around the house. "You are inventing a camera," Tomas told her.

It was Muybridge's work that most set her imagination running, The mix of photography as art and photography as engineering project, photography as machinery, invention. Muybridge took more than one hundred thousand pictures of animals and people in motion, beginning with a racehorse named Occident running on a track, to a man walking up an incline and then walking down an incline, two men wrestling, a woman walking and sprinkling water from a basin and turning around. There have been many published editions of his work, *Muybridge's Complete Human and Animal Locomotion,* which was also published separately as *Animals in Motion* and *The Human Figure in Motion*.

The point of Muybridge's photographs was to show how people and animals move, to actually see the physical evidence of muscles in action, how the muscles went about their work, to watch the muscles of the body move from photo to photo. To make movement visible, the human figures in his pictures are mostly naked or barely clothed: a man's penis and testicles are always covered but a woman is always naked.

Marie studied Muybridge's work, she took a lot of notes on his system, and after a few months she began to reproduce the project. She built twenty-four models of the camera that he used, though she cheated, she built box cameras that used 35mm film. The models were functional, and probably no clumsier than the originals. They used Kodak film and were triggered by light, not string.

There was an art gallery in the old French's building on Hochelaga Street east of Papineau. The building was rundown and had been taken over by small businesses and artists who kept studios there. The rent was cheap. Some artists lived in the building, though it was illegal. The Logos Gallery on the second floor agreed to host Marie's project as an installation, *After Muybridge*. She and Tomas set it all up for a three-day run over a long weekend. Muybridge's original project worked with a racehorse who ran across the field of the cameras, but Marie replaced the horse with dancers who moved as a pair across the field of vision. They wore unitards, like skin, almost as naked as Muybridge's people, and they turned their part of the project into dance, evoking a horse only by their movements, postures, the leader tall, the follower leaning slightly forward. They did not move in a straight line and crossed much more slowly than a racehorse would. They reproduced other series, too: fencers, a man running, a woman running. They wrestled. They danced. Marie wanted people to see the muscles in the dancers' bodies, the muscles in their thighs, their backs. During the afternoon, each day, Marie gave a lecture on the work of Muybridge, and showed the audience exactly how it worked, piece by piece. The dancers performed twice each day, and when they weren't on stage, Marie invited other people to walk, or run or dance, members of the audience. At night Marie and Tomas developed and printed photographs so they had examples to show the next day. If people came twice, they might see themselves. It was a combination of science and art, the history of technology. She talked about what Muybridge was thinking, and she imagined what the audience was thinking. She felt that perhaps his mind could have a moment in theirs.

She left out the part of Muybridge's story where he shot and killed a man named Harry Larkans. When he went to trial, Muybridge was found not guilty because, after all, Larkyns was sleeping with his wife. He shot his wife's lover, and people found that understandable.

On the last day of Marie's installation, a curator from the Science and Technology Museum attended a performance, and soon after the museum bought Marie's installation for $2,300. This was one of the larger sales anyone among their friends had made thus far, and some people were jealous. Of course, they said, It's not art. It's a high school science project.

Marie deposited her cheque and bought the used Ducati. She moved it into a rented garage a few blocks from home, tore it down completely, and brought it out the following spring, rebuilt, clean, with a let's-go somewhere hum. Tomas began to ride.

A Boy's Own Story

On a weekend afternoon, a man is standing at the corner of Saint-Denis and Mont-Royal waiting for the light to change. There are a lot of people spread around and Charlie is among them, standing near the man. While he's watching, a woman approaches the man from the other side. She stands in front of Charlie too, as though they are three people, a triangle, or maybe Charlie just doesn't exist for her. The woman seems quite a bit older than the other people on the street, although it's difficult to be certain because she's wearing a dark hooded sweatshirt, even on such a hot day, with the hood over her head and a mask pulled down to her chin. She is short and wide. She is holding up her left hand and her hand is shaking, she's shaking a lot. A serious tremor. She calls to the man. "Sir? Sir?" The man turns to her voice. "Can I have some money please?" He sighs, and twelve-year-old Charlie already understands the city humour in this. She caught the man looking and he can't just ignore her now. Charlie moves back a bit, but he would still like to see her face. The man reaches into his pocket and pulls out some money. There are three two-dollar coins, and with his other hand he picks out one to give to the woman.

"Can I have four dollars?" She takes the two. "Give me four dollars."

"No."

"Can I have four dollars please? I'm hungry."

"No. I have to keep some myself."

"Give me four dollars. I'm hungry." She's whining now. "This is my first two dollars today."

"No."

"Give me four dollars!"

"No! You give me back my two dollars."

She takes one step away from him. The light changes. The man crosses the street in the crowd, his body is tense, he's pissed.

The woman stands on the sidewalk, watching him, ignoring all the people around her. Charlie is still standing nearby. All the other people are ignoring her. "You fucking asswipe!"

Lorca and David worry about the way he goes off on his own. Charlie likes to wander out of his own life. This is not to say he doesn't love his parents, or that he doesn't have any friends and take pleasure in those friendships. He does all those things. But he also likes to explore. He's a Heyerdahl, after all, a lesser adventurer. He goes one day to the Botanical Gardens and stands outside because he doesn't have any money. He just watches. He has been a few times to Old Montreal, the Sailors' Church and the docks along de la Commune, the old stables, or he rides the bus to the ends of the island, Cartierville, the back river, or in the other direction, Pointe-aux-Trembles. He likes to walk around downtown—the pool hall on Alexander Street thrills him, it feels so dangerous he can't get over it, until they throw him out. People watching.

At seven-thirty in the morning, Charlie Heyerdahl enters the Outremont subway station on his way to school. He attends an alternative school in downtown Montreal, where if you were the school's principal you would be making those old jokes about attendance apparently being optional. At the subway station, Charlie falls into line behind a man and a woman, and when they come to the escalator, they slow down for a moment. Charlie happens to be watching the woman as they do this and he is struck by the look in her eyes. The man and the woman slow down, and she turns slightly toward the man and smiles. Charlie sees that smile in the woman's eyes, and her smile is quite lovely, although he would not say it that way. He does not know how to say it. He feels himself drawn to her. He is a boy struck at the momentary look in a woman's brown eyes just before she steps onto the escalator. He follows them down the long escalator, thinking about what he's just seen.

Really, it isn't much. A couple walked together to the subway station, and as they were getting on the escalator, the man hesitated for a moment to allow the woman to go ahead of him. At another time, the man might have held out his hand to her, *After you.* The woman, with the slightest gesture, acknowledged his politeness and smiled, *Thank you.* That's all he saw, what others might have noticed, but that doesn't explain the pleasure in the woman's eyes. If Charlie were a man, he might think, *Well, those people have had a nice morning, they're still warm.*

But Charlie isn't a man. He loses the couple in the crowd, but he's still thinking about the woman's eyes. What does that feel like? What is comparable to the look in her eyes? It seems to him a little like the feeling he has when he makes his mother laugh, or his father. Making his parents laugh does not feel the same as making his friends laugh. Lorca knows this, and she gives her laughter freely, but it is rare that Charlie makes his father laugh. Charlie decides that he will go to the metro station early tomorrow morning and wait to follow the woman and the man again, although he'll forget to do that, and they won't be there for him then anyway.

A Pause Inside the Circle

"This is the city that I love, these particular days."

It happens sometimes that two women meet through a man. One is his mother and the other becomes his wife. Of course, Marie is excited to have a daughter-in-law to care for (a daughter!), especially someone she likes, this attentive young woman with her cigarette jeans and her long black hair, that lovely smile, who is beginning her adult life, maybe a geographer (they don't imagine that one day years from now she'll be a beekeeper), but they are only coming to know each other, learning each other's attitudes and habits. They are slowly becoming friends and it's not so easy for adults to make new friendships. They planned to meet at a restaurant downtown for lunch. Marie walks along Sherbrooke Street. It's a warm spring day, people are opening up their bodies, relaxed, the students already in their summer clothes, dawdling, popcorn-horny, and Mount Royal is growing green over the buildings behind them.

They're hardly ever alone. They have known each

other less than two years and they still wonder sometimes what's on the other's mind. One thinks, *What is their life at home like? When there's no one else around?* The other wonders, and you can see the unsure gestures in her hands sometimes, *How does this woman think of my life with her son? Does she approve?* Marie comments that they both seem very happy and, with only that, Lorca is pleased.

Their conversations sometimes grow silent, but they are not uncomfortable together. When they part there is a sense of pleasure in the afternoons that they sometimes share. They walk a few blocks down to Sainte-Catherine Street and end up in the bookstore at the corner of Stanley. It's the busiest store, and the largest—three floors that are divided into nooks and corners here and there. They spend more than an hour here, going through the store floor by floor. They separate, follow their interests, looking back at each other across the room. It's curious for them to watch the other in that environment, how they stand out among strangers. And then they come back together, checking out the other's choices, the books in their hands, a handbook of time, a novel by John Irving, a biography of Galileo. There are rings on their fingers, six between the two of them.

o

On a cold winter day they come together in the kitchen with glasses of wine and Marie helps Lorca, who has been preparing dinner; there's a plate of vegetables with hummus to serve in the other room, with a wonderful meal already in the oven. The table is almost set, and while they work they talk about the past few weeks in their lives. They ask questions (men don't ask so many questions). They talk about their family; this is singular, as they are extensions of each other within that family. They share their thoughts on recent world events. They talk about food or politicians or even both at the same time, spices, or spicy music, the cold, or art, or money, or clothes. They talk about children, though one's child is an adult and now a parent himself. They don't talk much about him, that can be a touchy subject between a mother and a wife. He comes into the room once or twice, *Can I help you? No, it's all right, how's the baby?* Sometimes Marie, who drives a Volkswagen now with a shovel in the trunk, will talk about busses or airplanes. She'll talk about machinery, which Lorca likes to hear. It's a whole other world for her to imagine. She thinks of straight lines, blueprints, clean parts that work together in specific ways. She's a little jealous of that.

o

"Stop talking and swim."

Lorca and Marie are swimming across Lake Moreau. Charlie is six years old and wearing a life jacket and he is there in the water with them. He calls out about lunch, he calls out about fish nibbling at his toes, he calls out about things his father told him. "Mum," he calls. "Grandma." He spits water. He'd splash them if he could. "Wait for me. Don't go so far ahead."

Lorca and Marie look back waiting for him to catch up, and then begin to swim again, slow breaststroke, treading, laughing, drifting around him. "Stop talking, kid." They are all having a good time, the two women treading water and the little boy bobbing between them, turning back and forth a dozen metres from shore.

The day is perfect. Sunlight flecks off the water and warms their faces and shoulders. The water too is warm. It's quiet, there are a hundred cottages spread along the shore but there's hardly anyone else around this afternoon. The lake isn't very wide, and they usually swim the length of it, which stretches in a kind of V-shape, but this time they are only swimming across. Each of them has a pull-float on a rope attached to her ankle. This is mostly a show for Charlie's benefit. They are smooth swimmers, and they like to swim together, they can go a long way.

They swim back toward the house, around the lily pads, leaving Charlie on the dock with David, and they turn away to start again, taking the long route now. They like the time it takes to swim the length and back because it lets them swim into their own bodies. They are quiet for a long time, serious in what they're doing, but there's a small island, mostly rocky with a few trees, where they like to stop for a moment, resting in the water, chatting like sea lions. They like the way they feel moving across the lake, and they like the accomplishment that they share, and they like the way they feel when they're done. Someone gives them towels, lemonade, peaceful in the sun. Charlie always wants them.

Do You Live Alone?

Q.   Do you live alone?
No, I am married. No children. No pets.

Q.   How often are you alone?
Every day, at some point, in my body and certainly in my spirit.

Q.   Are you alone for hours at a time, or shorter periods (commuting, for example)?
I do have commuting time to myself, though I don't consider that being alone. I am often alone in the evening. I keep a journal and there are times when I feel I am alone even when other people are nearby when I'm writing in the journal.

Q.   Do you sleep alone?
Rarely.

Q.   Do you sleep better with someone else, or alone? Does it matter one way or the other?
Yes. I sleep better with someone else in my bed, as long as we are not angry with each other.

Q.   If you are alone for more than an hour, what do you like to do?
I am rebuilding a motorcycle and I like to be alone with that, though sometimes I like to just hang around the apartment. I don't think of it as a hobby.

Q.   Do you like silence when you're alone?
There are days when I like silence very much, but when I'm working I like to listen to music. Charlebois. Diane Dufresne.

Q.   Pastimes? Do you like music? Do you watch television? Do you read books?   ·
Motorcycles. Books. Music (oh, my sweet Charlebois). Art.

Q.   Are you ever alone for two days or more at a time? What's that like?
The only thing that keeps me from becoming someone else (could this mean becoming myself?) is the expectation of the other's return.

o

Marie and Tim were on Park Avenue. She had walked up from Sherbrooke and he left the studio to meet her at the corner of Villeneuve, near the Dairy Queen. He was still in his painting clothes, tall and rumpled and splattered. In her diary she wrote, *I suppose I unkemp him,* not serious about it, playing with the words. She was learning not to see him as a reflection of herself. They were walking on Park near Fairmont Street. Tim was grumpy. The work wasn't going well. He wanted a glass of beer, or two or three, so they were walking north in the direction of Saint-Viateur. They were talking about the day so far, though without interest. Neither had much to say. There was a strip club there on the east side of Park, EXXX-uberance, or something like that, many Xs, sex and alcohol, just across the street from where they were walking, and at a moment when traffic was stopped Tim led her through the cars to cross the street. He was heading straight into the club, but she stopped on the sidewalk. He looked back. "I'm not going in there." Marie laughed, like he must have been kidding.

He reached for her hand. "We'll just have a drink," he said, and turned back to pull her inside. Three enormous pictures covered the front of the club, the huge windows that face the sidewalk where they stood, and where people pass by all day. They were walking by her. The posters were seven or eight feet high, naked women in a sort of faux jungle setting, their breasts covered by the green leaves of plants. The lush garden of the pictures was many years old and the colours were faded and dull, everything turning yellow in the sun. Marie pulled her hand away and she was grateful that Tim didn't argue. He nodded. He did accept it. They continued walking a few blocks and sat in another bar on Saint-Viateur. *I couldn't understand why he would try to bring me there. Couldn't he see why I wouldn't go in? Who does he think I am?* They chatted a little at the table, but mainly sat in silence. They looked at the televisions bolted to the walls around the room. It was Saturday afternoon and there was a soccer game on.

Who does he think I am?

"Do you go there often?"

He answered in a low voice—*No*—with an annoyed tone. It made her want to cry.

Later Tim apologized. They walked home. He apologized again. "Never mind, it's forgotten," she said. "It's almost forgotten," she said. *Really*, she told herself, *this is nothing*. Right? It's always nothing. *But I don't like this. It is nothing!* She prepared supper and they watched television. They both stayed in for the night. Make-up sex, fitful sleep.

○

Divorce is difficult but it's not so unusual. It's just change, it happens all the time. One third of all marriages end in divorce, and Monday is the day that most people begin seriously considering divorce, the morning after yet another weekend. Marie left one husband and then married another. This is the simplest way to say it. A few words that overlook the yo-yo of her emotions at the time. Marie married one man and then she took another, without a span of time between the two relationships—that is, without a period alone to herself, only those daily hours that had always been hers. She had faith in the classical tradition, intuitive, furnished, heteronormative: wife and husband. She was mistaken in her expectations of Timothée, but not Tomas. Her code was exactly what he needed, ample, inclusive, like a mirror as big as a wall, bold and still. Tomas too began sometimes to think of the future, and they could actually feel they knew the future, how they would fit. Tomas was a beginner who didn't realize he was just beginning, he had an island past to somewhat slowly un-intuit, that the best he could hope for was mystery, that there was no explanation. Tomas wrapped himself inside Marie, he whispered in her ear, *I am your knight in shining armour, hobo armour*. They had a home on Drolet Street with the front step right on the sidewalk. He called down the hall, *Have you seen my keys?* They constructed a variant on the domesticity Marie had grown up within. Books all over the house, and photographs, matted and framed, a study upstairs, a darkroom in the basement, and a garage down the street. There was a Nokogiri saw on her desk, and she played with it like a feather in her hand, pulling the teeth across the oak desk unconsciously, leaving grooves. She admired coping saws too. *Can you cope? Can you cope?* A gear box in pieces on a pine shelf. Early Mac computers, Performas. They had a child and named him David, there was a swing on the tree in the back yard and a park across the street. Schools.

Gerbils. A growing boy. They celebrated events. They were attractive young classicists. Sometimes it turns out well.

The night her parents met Tomas, they wondered what she saw in that kind of boy? The differences between Timothée and Tomas were not immediately appreciable. *She's an engineer! Our daughter can build subways! Bridges! She builds machines! Oh, those motorcycles…*

Photography and the Lost Soul

Taking a photograph, or thousands of photographs, should not be confused with being alive. The photographer is alive, but the camera is held between the photographer and the subject. Distance for the observer. Photographer as interpreter, or photography as curtain or shield.

We each make about thirty-five thousand decisions in the span of one day, and we have between sixty thousand and eighty thousand ideas or thoughts. Of all those thoughts and ideas, ninety-five percent are thoughts and ideas we already had the day before, and most of them we had the day before that too. So there's not much new, but we do go on and on. And they say we do all this deciding and thinking using only about ten percent of our brain cells. We are remarkable and frail.

Taking a photograph, or even many photographs, is not the same as being alive, but this is only idle criticism, albeit often expressed. We underline the distinction between participant and observer. A voyeur at the window, looking through a screen. The active photographer in a passive role, as though there were only one or the other, as though many strands were not always entwined. The camera is held between the photographer and the subject, like a handful of fog. See the photographer leaning forward into the mechanical cloud of the camera, seeing how the light falls on the subject, checking the focus, the frame. The photographer is participating in what, exactly? Is it anything more than the act of making an image, maybe an image of a woman in a room with a white background and a beautiful silk scarf over her eyes, her head turned slightly to one side as though she is listening, and that turning of her head seems to emphasize the fact that she can't see. Maybe it's an image that means nothing but is just striking to look at. Can images mean nothing? Maybe it's an image that could sell a Chevrolet, or an expensive brand of bourbon. Who is the voyeur, the photographer or the person looking over the photographer's shoulder? What is the nature of images? Their language?

Sunday, June 12, 1976. T. strikes me as a bit of a lost soul. "What does it mean to say that a person is a lost soul?" he asked me. He was joking, he said. "Who says so? Lost how?" We were walking together and he stopped and looked up and down the street, quite gentlemanly in manner. "Is a lost soul a person who cannot find the way?" he asked, making us both laugh. "Lost in the city, like, *Uh oh, what street am I on? What strange neighbourhood is this?*" It's in his spirit that he seems a bit lost, I think, lost among everyone else. I pretended to trip over my feet, a stumbling, bumbling soul. I exaggerated. "You are a soul on a vast plain," I said. I was not unladylike. "Or on a little boat in the middle of the ocean. You cannot see where it ends. Does that feel like you?" I asked him, and he didn't have much to respond. "Perhaps you're not sure how to proceed?" I was holding his arm, which I should not do in public, but I wanted him to be sure this was a friendly conversation. He squeezed my hand tighter. "What of the soul alone in a vast field who is not looking to see where it ends at all?" he asked finally. "A soul alone in a field, a vast terrain—as busy as the ocean—and he's not looking for any horizon.... Is he not lost at all?"

○

A nice pair of tall leather boots have been left neatly side by side on the sidewalk near a tree on Mont-Royal Avenue. Traffic is busy, and many people walk by the boots. Tomas is a moderate soul who also walks right by, and this is another afternoon with nothing to do but walk. He throws whole days away and he worries sometimes about that, but still he throws whole days away. Tomas has a kind of poor-boy aura going on in his faded chinos and hardware-store shirt. A camera bag hangs across his shoulder and a Nikon is slung loosely around his neck.

Tomas climbs the stairs to Boulet Danse and asks if he can rent a studio. He chats with the girl at the counter about what's available, their prices. Of course the only studio left is the most expensive, sixty-eight dollars an hour. While he's paying, Tomas tells her a joke that falls flat and he has the urge to explain it to her, to try to tell it again, but he doesn't. He is very self-conscious and imagines that she is wondering what he's doing there, though he knows she is probably not thinking of him at all. The girl is clearly a dancer, even the way she's dressed, working at the counter, he imagines that she is working for studio time, time for time, and he very clearly is not a dancer. The room is one of the largest, with a capacity of twenty-six people. He is alone. One long wall is a mirror, floor to ceiling, the length of the room, with a heavy curtain partially closed. The wall facing the mirror is all windows that look out over Mont-Royal and the building across the street. The other walls are white. There is a big clock in the corner near the door to remind him of the time. There is no window in the door. Tomas is not a dancer, but he has been here a couple of times for photography projects, to work with the light from those walls of windows, the mirror. He first came here with a woman named Lydie, who brought him to the studios because she wanted to rehearse and then to show him what she was working on. Tomas had held a book in his hands and watched Lydie. While he watched her he thought about fucking right there on that big wooden floor in front of the wall of mirror. It would have been fun, but he wasn't bold enough to suggest it.

The studio has a great sound system, a Marshall. The amplifier is built into the wall near the door. Tomas takes off his shoes and socks. He takes off his shirt. He slides in a cassette of Renaissance choir music. He turns the volume up very high and the music explodes from all four corners, from speakers in the ceiling. He can feel the sound touch his body. The music is playing and it feels like he's in an empty church, he walks slowly around the studio. He is trying not to look in the mirror. He walks diagonally, he walks in loops. He changes directions, speeds. He hops. He stamps his feet on the beautiful hardwood floor. He takes long hard steps, stomps, then a long step and then a short step, a skip. He stretches his fingers, his arms. The music has no relation with what he is doing now, but the music is so loud and the room is so big that he forgets himself, he loses himself, as though he's wandering in another city. He has been set free of everything, free of being known.

Tomas lies down on the floor and rolls around. He flips from his back to his chest, then back again. He pulls his body around the floor on his elbows, he drags himself, he pushes his body with his feet, pushes with his toes. He hears the choir singing the word *Dei*. He lies on his back with his arms stretched wide and then flips onto his chest, slapping his hand on the floor, hard. He does this so many times his hands hurt and still he continues.

He rises. He doesn't look at the mirror, it's no longer a factor for him. He's not shy anymore. He stands at one corner of the room and begins crossing slowly, he leans forward with his arms hanging down and begins swinging them back and forth, sweeping, as though his arms were the strings of a mop or the felt straps flapping down in a car wash. He swings his whole body from side to side, his arms flopping like that from side to side. He is happy. The choir is singing in unison now. Even a simple gesture welcomes variations. How will he hold his body, leaning forward, tilting back? He moves sideways across the room. He moves fast, he moves slowly. For a little while, for forty-five minutes, he is only who he is.

When the time is up, he pulls out the cassette and turns off the system. Then he sits on a metal chair and puts on his shoes, his shirt. He is breathing heavily. A group of students come in to use the room after him. They barely acknowledge his presence.

On the way out he says goodbye to the girl at the counter and thanks her. *You're welcome*, she says. At the door he turns and comes back. "Do you have cameras?" he asks, "inside the rooms? It's not that I'm doing anything wrong. I just wonder whether I should be embarrassed or not."

This makes her laugh. She is standing now across the counter. A perfect girl, sleek as a line of thread, long black hair tied in a ponytail. She is generous. "No, you don't have to be embarrassed at all."

"Thank you," he says again, and goes out into the street.

A Good Day in Four Parts

A dog is running under a frisbee and leaps into the air as the disc arcs down. Marie and Tomas are eating ice cream on a bench in the park. "When I was eleven years old," Marie says, "I was on the swim team at the Cartierville boating club on the Rivière des Prairies. My family were members, though we didn't have a boat. We used the pool and had lunch or dinner there. Every year, the swim team took part in a fundraiser for charity and we all had to go out to find people who would sponsor us. The sponsors were asked to make a donation based on the number of laps of the pool we each did. I asked all my relatives and I went to my neighbours. People I hardly knew sponsored me and some just pledged five dollars, or three dollars, or else twenty-five cents or fifty cents a lap, but some of my relatives pledged a dollar a lap. I had a lot of sponsors. I went to all the houses for blocks around. My father came with me and waited on the sidewalk. I was very serious. I was all in for it."

"How many laps did you do?"

She laughs. "Ninety-eight! People freaked out. 'I'm not giving you a hundred dollars!' They made deals with me. My uncles! They gave me ten dollars, or twenty dollars. Imagine, adults bargaining with a little girl. I was quite hurt and I really tried to hold them to their pledges. My father said to forget about it, but it mattered to me. I wanted to be the one who raised the most money."

"It was their own fault. They should have asked you what to expect first. That's what I would do." Tomas holds open the palms of his hands, *it's obvious*. Two dogs are chasing down frisbees; he could take pictures of odd dog-shapes flying through the air. He points out the dogs to her. "So, you're competitive."

Marie squints at him and shrugs. "That's true. I do like to win."

o

It was May but Marie was wearing a cotton dress and sandals, and a small leather bag across her shoulders. In this city, the seasons can change over a weekend and people come out like zombies to the light. They wait at bus stops with their faces turned to the sun, lizards on a rock. This was the fifth time that Tomas and Marie were meeting, and the first time they had a few hours together by themselves. This was the beginning, a couple of years before their trip across the country. They had run into each other on Mont-Royal. It's a lively street, engineers and photographers and flower children and the people with the wise-guy mouths and the drug dealers. *Hash?* Cars and pedestrians and bicycles, people dressed in jeans or dresses or nose rings or chains, everyone is welcome on a warm Sunday afternoon. *Pot?* Marie was coming out of the bookstore called Bonheur d'occasion, and there was Tomas on the sidewalk. They didn't know each other very well, but still it was a welcome surprise to run into each other. Marie had bought a used Chilton motorcycle manual, and he asked about that. "Is that for you? Are you interested in motorcycles?" He smiled like he found her hobby amusing or surprising, but she was used to that.

"Yes, I do like motorcycles a lot." She held the book out in her hands. "I'm interested in machinery." The book was functional, and extremely used, the pages curled or torn and stained with grease. "It was in the fifty-cent bin." Marie was wearing four rings on her hands that day, and bracelets on one wrist. She wore a wedding ring, and she had a silver ring with a red stone on her left thumb. This is some of what he noticed; her hands, her fingers. They had only met a few times, but still they felt friendly, familiar. She had thought of Tomas as quiet, but he was less tentative alone with her on the sidewalk. She decided that he just stood back in groups, a listener, observer. He was a photographer, after all. She liked that he didn't react to all conversation by turning it back to himself, tying it to his own life. There could be quiet between them. And she liked it that he wasn't looking off at whatever was going on down the street. "What about you?" she asked, "do you like motorcycles?"

"I've never even been on a motorcycle."

"That's too bad for you. Would you be afraid?"

"I don't think so. Probably not; it's just a bicycle with a motor."

She smiled at that. "You don't know what you're talking about."

"Yes, I know. I do that."

Someone had left a pair of red leather boots near a small tree the city had planted by the sidewalk, and Tomas stopped. He asked Marie to stand beside the boots, the left side, then on the right side. He overdid it. He was trying to entertain her. He ran across the street through traffic, waving, this way, that way. He ran back, holding his camera in his hand. He took the pictures of the boots with her legs beside them. He ran back again. She watched him handle the camera, the bones in his fingers, his knuckles.

"Which way are you going?" he asked her. "Can I walk with you?"

"Yes, sure."

"Wait!" He turned back slightly. "Do you want a pair of boots? I'll carry them for you if you'd like."

"No, but thank you," she said. "You're very chivalrous."

Although she had known of his work for almost two years, and he had known of her for almost the same time, they had only really met six months earlier, and their paths had crossed only a few times since then, always with other people—at a gallery, a theatre, a New Year's party. They would speak for a few minutes or stand in a circle with drinks in their hands. Marie was married to Timothée Villiers, who Tomas knew a little better than he did Marie. Tomas asked about Tim, more as a formality, to acknowledge that she was married than out of any real curiosity, and Marie replied that Tim was fine. She talked about the new work that he was doing. "When he's not teaching, he's in the studio all the time." She watched Tomas. "Your friend Munk is there working with him a lot these days."

"Yes, I know Munk pretty well, but I didn't know he was a painter."

"No, he isn't a painter, but he's a good carpenter. Tim is working on a series of large sculptures and the maquettes are made of wood, plywood, the lamination is part of the sculpture, and Munk is doing the actual woodworking. Tim draws the plans and Munk makes the sculpture. It's a Renaissance arrangement, master and craftsman. Munk has brought a lot of tools over to the studio and he's set himself up like he's going to be there for a while, power tools and boxes, and two buckets of clamps and hammers and screwdrivers. He owns a beautiful Japanese handsaw that makes very fine cuts. He carries it in a folding leather case, like a jewel. Munk's a jeweller." This idea stops her for a moment, she'd like to talk about Munk's tools, the way he takes care of his tools. She says that Tim complains about Munk getting sawdust all over everything, all over his paintings, but from what she's seen, Munk cleans up all the time. He's diligent. "They drink beer until midnight and Tim complains, or maybe he just complains when he gets home."

They stopped talking about Marie's husband. Tomas assumed she did not know that often Timothée had one or two younger women with him in the studio, students, among others. Everyone else knew. Tomas had heard it from Munk, the gossip, but he didn't mention it now. He walked west with her along Mont-Royal toward the park.

Marie worked in civil engineering; she had to explain to him what that meant. At the time, her company was working on a project to produce 368 subway cars for the city of Philadelphia, and she talked about her part with the design team. He was impressed, and he felt inadequate compared to her, childish. She was accomplished, a married woman. "You build subway cars!"

"No!" She laughed. "I don't build them." In her own mind she was quite ordinary. "My company has twelve thousand employees; I'm just a cog in the machine." She often felt that she was living like a fifty-year-old woman, she said, but Tomas disagreed.

"No, I don't see that."

They walked by the Boulet Danse Studio, but Tomas did not tell her about the hour he had spent before running into her, nor did he show her how to do the wading bird dance he'd invented, right there on the sidewalk, waving his arms around. It wasn't until a year later that he'd take her up there, the two of them dancing like wading birds, watching each other in the mirror, checking around for a camera.

They talked about the parts of cameras. Marie was interested in how a camera works, light and glass, mirrors; she would have liked to open it up. She asked how he thinks about photography. "What do you like to photograph?" There were difficult questions. "What are the aesthetics of your work? How do you feel about photographing people?" He talked about the general strike, three years ago already, photographing the strikers, the emotions on their faces. He told her about a bearded man's face frozen in a shout, his tight mouth, and he told her how much money he made for that picture. Even in his most crowded group pictures, there is usually a particular person who stands out, something about that person becomes the root of the picture, or maybe it's the flight of the picture. The one who brings it to life. "It's always something inside the picture, a person, an expression, a gesture, or the way a body seems to be moving. There is a picture of a person in pain, a grimace; a photo of four policemen beating someone on the ground with batons, the person's legs and arms in the air, trying to block them. When you look at the pictures you can't help but look for the policemen's eyes. What do people see? Do they wonder, *Would I be that kind of person?* What is photography for? To say, *Look at this.* Documentation? To convey a personal sense of the world through a collection of images?"

Tomas told her about his photograph *Roger on his Way to Visit Claire*. On the metro near Alexis Nihon Plaza, Tomas had met a man with a string tie and an old herringbonc jacket, big shoes and bony ankles. He looked like a homeless man who had dressed up. He seemed anxious, twitchy. He looked at Tomas, and when Tomas looked back at him, the man smiled. "I'm going to visit Claire." In the station, Tomas took his picture and gave him ten dollars to bring her flowers. It was a story that pleased Marie.

"I'd like to see that picture." He took the camera off

and hung it around her neck.

She took pictures as they walked, holding the camera in both hands. A cat in a third-floor window. A storefront filled with wooden toys, a tall children's crane made of wood and a red and white airplane. Seven birds. People standing at a street corner waiting for the light to change. She was interested in the way a woman kept tapping the toe of her shoe on the ground behind her. Matter becomes energy. She took two pictures of Tomas.

They sat on a bench with the tennis courts behind them, enjoying the sounds of the game, the balls against the racquets and the squeaking shoes. There were a few photographs that Tomas would have liked to take, the details of her neck, loose strands of her hair, the line of her collarbone, but he left the camera alone on the bench. There was a vaccination scar on her left shoulder. When they were quiet, she had a look on her face that made him want to ask, *What are you thinking?* To the left of them there was a baseball diamond, and a softball diamond to their right, closer to the street. If they walked south a little, they would have come to a football field, artificial turf with game lights and fences. Nearby there is a children's playground, a picnic area, and across the road, volleyball courts. "All that's missing here," Marie said, "is a good swimming pool."

○

An hour later they were sitting together on a wooden bench near a row of tennis courts in Jeanne Mance Park.

"My father was a fisherman," Tomas said. "And he was an alcoholic, which is not so unusual. They go together. A fisherman needs to drink, and the hard hours burn off the alcohol. My father worked on other people's boats; he didn't have his own. He also liked horse racing—gambling—and he taught me to like it too."

They were eating ice cream near the tennis courts. It was a day to relax, and the ice cream cones were a nice summery activity, and oddly intimate. Taste. Cold on their tongues on a warm day. Tomas began to tell her a story about his father. About horses and gambling, but really, it was about his father. The fence rattled near them whenever a ball smacked it, not close enough to make them duck. He was holding her motorcycle book in his hands, flipping the pages, looking at illustrations.

"My father would drive to the racetrack in Summerside, and when I was eleven he started taking me with him. It was about an hour's drive and sometimes we'd stay there overnight at a motel." Tomas was just talking, enjoying this afternoon with Marie, a couple of hours, watching people in the park, watching her. Marie watching him too. They were watching each other, close together, the camera and the book between them, there was no rush to the afternoon. Shoes squeaked on the tennis courts. Someone missed a ball and called, *Shit*. Tomas left out the nasty parts of his story. He didn't tell her that his father would leave him alone in the room with the television and a chicken and Coke. *Lock the door, boyo*. Then he'd come back in the middle of the night, plastered, and Tomas would pretend to be asleep. *Hey boyo*.

There was a catalpa tree between the bench and the courts, eight or nine metres high, and it was already beginning to flower; they could smell the flowers in the air. Marie said that soon catalpa pods and seeds would be falling onto the tennis courts, annoying everyone, a mess to sweep up.

A woman passed by with a baby in a stroller and a dog beside her. "Even the dogs are pleased today," Marie said, "and why not."

One of the players behind them called out *Sorry*. That happened as often as someone yelling *Shit. Merde*. It seemed it could be a difficult game. "I was too young to go into the track, so I waited outside. My father would come out between races. A lot of people only go for the Daily Double, the first two races, and then they leave. I'd hang around the gate and when they came out after the second race I'd ask them for their programs and then I'd sell the programs for fifty cents to people who were just coming into the track. When my dad came over to see me, if I had collected two dollars, we'd go over the next race and I'd pick a horse to bet on and he'd take my money and make my bet."

He was watching her eyes as she listened to him. She was imagining the boy and his father discussing horses. He had her attention. She asked how he chose a horse, how much did he win.

"I hardly ever won anything, maybe a dollar or two, but he'd come out and give me my losing ticket, which I kept. I saved all those tickets in an envelope for a long time, until I left home.

"Oh, I like this story," she said, and suddenly he remembered the night of his vernissage and the way she'd draw in a breath with people around her and then her words would gush out. This afternoon the sentences didn't pour out, she was calm and bright. Tomas was smiling. Marie teased him: "Little gambler boy. Do you still gamble?"

"I didn't know anything about horses, and I don't now either." He shook his head. "I don't gamble. My father gave me advice, but mostly I chose by name. Sometimes I could watch the horses through the slats in the fence, and then I'd pick one that looked good to me, or that had the coolest colours, or was breathing heavy"—Tomas raised back his head—"big open nostrils." He laughed. "It was probably a bad sign, to be breathing heavily before the race. Anyway, I picked what I picked. I don't know that my dad did so much better than me."

He said that she should see these tennis courts under the lights at night, "The most beautiful colours to photograph," and she said yes, she'd played there a few times in the past.

"I loved my dad on days when I won a race. Once I won enough to pay for our dinner. We had burgers."

○

In one of the pictures Tomas took of her that day, Marie is already across the street, walking away. For him, taking a picture can be a cognitive function: he has the image to help him think. The camera orients him by all it leaves out. Some people learn by being told, but others learn through experience. One is not always better than the other, although one is usually slower than the other, which may count against it.

Marie's shoulders seem slender in the photo but her back is quite straight, and the line of her back has meaning for Tomas when he looks. He can see vigour. That's what the picture suggests to him. He stood on the sidewalk, watching like a man in a story about a forest. He took the picture. Sometimes we understand intuitively; if we want to lead a better life we are drawn to what we need to do. And already he knew he would need to be close to her. Marie could sense how he felt, she was not unaffected by the attraction, but it made her uncomfortable and she turned away. In her diary that evening all she wrote was, *long walk with T.* While she continued to think of him often, she didn't write about him very much at all, and when she did she referred to him in code, as T.

In Tomas's picture she is carrying the motorcycle manual in her left hand. Her purse hangs across her body from her right shoulder to her left side, and in her right hand the tips of her index finger and her thumb are touching, forming a circle. For a while he finds this the most curious thing about her. Why does she walk like that? What is the circle she is closing? They had not yet touched each other.

o

Her aunt was reading Marie's tea leaves in a delicate china cup. "Oh dear, I'm not very good at this." Marie went to see a fortune teller who swirled her up in a crystal ball, the ball told the woman everything, though she skipped over the sordid details. A woman read her tarot cards in a dark room that smelled like sandalwood. They all told her what she already knew. "I see a second man coming to you here. He might be a fisherman."

"A fisherman's son." She looked away. "I don't believe in this."

"Nevertheless."

The I Ching and two fortune cookies both said the same thing. *You know what's up.*

She filled many pages of her diaries with secret wondering, thinking privately, looking for order. But it seemed simple; she would either have to adjust her beliefs to accommodate her life, marriage or Tomas, or adjust her life to accommodate her beliefs. *I'm not this sort of person, to make this choice.* But she turned to Tomas anyway.

He is making her a believer. He kneels by the bed and draws Marie toward him with his hands. Later, while she's dressing he says, *Just stay*, and she lingers for a little while longer, making the choice, though eventually she does leave. She can't say for how long she will continue to leave like this. It has been eight, nine months, and she knows her future will be here, this is becoming her home—*Though we need a bigger place.* She has no one to talk to about how this sort of thing works, but time comes to help resolve the dilemma. They are together more often, and frequently now they go outside, sharing what pleases them. Their friends begin to notice Marie and Tomas laughing on a street corner in the evening, sitting in a restaurant. The friends lean to each other, gossiping. Or they watch Marie and Tomas in a crowded room, maybe they are standing in separate groups but glancing over toward each other. People keep looking, and the attentive ones can see what they are looking at. Marie knows what they can see. She has already changed her life, and her beliefs, though she has yet to say it out loud. But when does Tim begin to see, before or after Marie says the words? When she finally tells him, does he really just nod, *Yes, huh, so I guess we're both full of shit*? How often are people that honest?

So it happens that at three a.m. on a cold morning in February, Marie Lextase lets herself into Tomas Heyerdahl's small apartment. He wakes and goes sleepily to her, and just like that it's done. She is standing inside the door. She is crying. He takes off her coat and pulls it over his own shoulders. At first they don't speak. She is crying softly but they are excited too. He tries to wrap them both in her coat together. The skin rejoices.

Suppose you are Timothée Villiers. You are a promising young artist, only in your thirties and your work is already becoming recognized in various cities across the country—you have a few famous friends in New York City, even in Vienna, an invitation from the Schiele school. You are a young man who has been married to an accomplished and attractive woman for about a year and a half. There was a great celebration at your wedding, so many friends dancing late into the night, drunk. Suppose now that you have a home with your wife and a loft studio for you and your friends, not too far from the university where you are a part-time professor. Your students like you and some of your students like you very much, as you do a few of them. You like some people inappropriately, that's true, but you're enjoying your life. Suppose that one Saturday afternoon your wife, who is a person with more depth of consciousness than you, bumps into an acquaintance on Mont-Royal Avenue where she has been shopping in a used bookstore. She hardly knows this person, he's kind of a peripheral guy, yet after meeting him—and maybe it has something to do with meeting him the way she does, the freedom of being alone on a crowded sidewalk on a warm, relaxed afternoon—she slowly, or not so slowly but over a period of months, enters into an enraptured relationship with him. And she leaves you. Your wife divorces you. Are you surprised? Didn't you notice the signs? Would you ask, *What is my part in this?* Does it matter?

○

The first time he took her picture naked was about six months after their tennis court afternoon, the long walk of Marie with T. They were in his apartment, his two rooms. He had a small round glass table with a metal frame and two matching metal chairs, there was a bed. He was a man who lived with old patio furniture that he'd bought in an alley, and a large darkroom. It interested her that he seemed so selective in what he cared about, or that there was so little he seemed to care about. Marie left her boots by the door, and hung her coat and scarf on a hook and put her mittens in the sleeve. It was a month before Christmas. A string of white lights hung from the ceiling to the floor in one corner of the room. He had taken a picture of her coming in the door one day and pinned it on the wall near the door. There was a cloth reindeer also hanging from one of the pins. She dropped her bracelets onto the glass table. She left her smell on one side of the bed.

One afternoon they were fucking and she rolled up on top of him, she was sitting straight, moving him into her, and he reached for the camera on the floor nearby. He took the pictures without looking, without focus. He held the camera out in one hand and then moved it to the other. He pointed the camera from his waist. She could see what he was doing and she took it as a game. For a moment she posed, leaning back, ironic, but then the camera just became another element, the pleasure of being looked at.

The pictures were all out of focus, and when he printed them he cranked them a little further. She looked like an apparition, a ghost of a person. He printed three black and white pictures, two very large and one small square photo. He put the small one in a frame. He hung them all on the wall and the next time she came over he asked her what she thought. "Well, it isn't me," she said. "They are very nice pictures, this one is like something from a seance, no? It's neo-expressionism." She didn't mind her own nudity. "It doesn't look like me at all, does it?"

Ways to Know the Future

By salt, by sand, by barley, by walking, by burning coals, by flowers, by altars, by one's own shoulders, by wind, by frogs, by smoke, by sleepiness, by thunder, by burning, by things on paper, by cookies, by the Iliad, by apt occasion, by comet tails, by shells, by wine, by demons, by trees, by second glances, by dripping blood, by dreams, by fractals, by laughter, by footprints, by rice, by words, by spots on the skin, by moles and blemishes, by foolishness, by summoning damned souls, by eyes or teeth, by the howling of dogs, by dreams, by eggs, by the word *yes*, by pebbles, by fear, by light, by observing the patterns produced by a collection of human hair, by looking over one's shoulder, by shoes, by shadows, by excrement, by burning straw, by skulls, by the soles of one's feet, by tea, by fashion, by the wind in the trees, by things found on the road, by all forms of creature behaviour, by one's own soul, by umbilical cords.

Pattern Days

Sometimes the best adventures are things that happen to other people. Lorca reached her hand across the table as though to touch David's cheek. She was already amused. "My tired boy." They stood up, clearing dishes. It was Sunday night, and everything was ready for Monday.

The previous Saturday, a warm late-August morning, David, Tomas, and David's friend Edward had driven in one car to Eddie's cottage near Sainte-Adèle. It was only an hour from the city, and not far from Lorca's childhood home, a fair-sized clapboard house down a hill from the highway, through spruce and birch into a clearing. They parked near the door. There were three bedrooms with old, soft mattresses, a wood stove, and a screened-in porch. The house had a good sound system but no television. There was a lake just twenty metres from the front door, with a floating dock and a rowboat. The three of them had planned to stay overnight and they had brought food and drink, cases of beer and a bottle of Balvenie, Caribbean Cask (they were wasting good scotch), and tabs of lysergic acid diethylamide, that is, a drug that can alter a person's perception of reality and vividly distort the senses.

Lorca was looking forward to hearing about it. David had returned all touchy-feely, following her around like a puppy. She remarked that he looked exhausted, and he closed his eyes, smiled. It was Sunday night and David had come home. The three of them—Lorca, David, and Charlie—ate dinner. They talked about the country, fishing, a rowboat, traffic. Lorca made tea, and Charlie went to watch TV. David stood here and there, in no hurry to do anything, leaving the room and coming back to her. It made her wonder what was going on with him.

"We brought everything into the house, got ourselves settled. We had a beer and then we dropped acid. I shared a tab with Dad.

"It was really too amazing to ever describe properly. The world is very beautiful; that's a cliché but we don't see it. People take things for granted. We hung around the house listening to music and talking, though you get really focused, if you're listening to music you're not talking, or you talk and you don't listen to music. We were having a good time, and I realized that it wasn't bad, nothing terrible was going to happen. We went outside and just walked around.

"Everything is stunning." David spread his hands wide, trying to indicate the breadth of how beautiful it all was. "Really stunning!"

"Let's go outside," Lorca said, thinking about Charlie, "bring your tea outside." The way she said it, she could have laughed, talking like he was recovering from an illness.

"I don't know how to explain it," he said. "Every single thing is so itself." He looked into her eyes. "Everything has its own essence, separate from every other thing around it." He moved his hand across in front of himself and followed it with his eyes. "Your focus just goes from one thing to the next. There's no blur. Everything stands out, leaf by leaf, object by object. Everything is alive in itself."

David and his father and Eddie had stood at the edge of the lake for a long time. There were so many birds around them, and they were so noisy, someone remarked that the birds were stoned too. They listened to water lapping at the side of the dock. There was a dragonfly in the air near them. Two dragonflies. A cloud in the sky. Everything was stoned! Water lilies were floating, waving. The birch trees were stoned! They watched people at the other cottages, they waved to people in boats, saying hello. Weird, it seemed weird. They were a little paranoid that other people might think it was strange, three guys standing by the lake, but Eddie said it was fine. "Nothing's wrong." They weren't crazy.

"We did go out in the rowboat, which was ridiculous. You would have laughed at that. Dad was bailing with a yogurt container. Eddie rowing. Things can take a very long time on acid. I don't know how long things take, but it doesn't matter anyway. We'd all be talking or else not talking at all. You can get completely paranoid and then be cured of it, all in a few seconds. We were having a good time, but none of us could row the boat properly and it took a long time just to get back to shore, laughing at ourselves, pathetic."

She put the tea bag on the edge of a little table, listening to David. He was getting into it. "Water would splash up and hit my face and I'd be like, *Oh my God!*" He shook his head as though ducking from the water, making her laugh loud enough that the neighbours could hear. *Ssh.*

He was enjoying himself now, telling the story. "We had a beer inside the house and my dad put a bucket of water on the floor. He took a green garbage bag and tied a lot of knots in it and then hung it from a string attached to a beam in the ceiling. He lit the bag on fire and the three of us sat there watching the drops of melting plastic fall into the bucket of water, *zzt, zzzzt.*" He was laughing and Lorca said *You could have burnt the house down*, and David stopped, *Yes, that's true*, but he said they never thought of that. "It was mind-blowing," he said. "Now I understand the 1960s."

"We drove into Sainte-Adèle to eat. Eddie drove, though I would have liked to. It would have been completely safe. We went to a restaurant up the hill near the Chantecler Hotel and put on a show for the waitress. Eddie had to park the car on the hill and we must have spent twenty minutes worrying about the parking brake and what if the car rolls down the hill. Then you should have seen us walking up the hill; it felt like climbing a cliff. In the bar we all fell in love with the waitress. She was quite attractive, beautiful brown eyes, though we were especially receptive. The beer was so good, cold, cold, cold, but

I ordered spaghetti and then I couldn't eat it. I had a few bites but I couldn't chew it. It wouldn't chew." He made a disgusted face. "*Wlaug*. I couldn't even look at it. I asked her for ice cream. The waitress must have seen this kind of thing before because she figured out what was going on pretty quick, and then she just got into it and played around with us. She pointed at dad, *He's your father?* I said, *Yeah, I'm looking after him*. We were laughing a lot, and there were some other customers there who could hear us and they were laughing too. I think everyone knew we were zonked and it didn't bother them, we were entertaining them."

"We drove back in the blackest night ever, hung out, and then just slept it off."

"How much tip did you leave?"

He shook his head. "I don't even know." He touched her leg. "You and I should get high together. We'll get stoned and go dancing."

David didn't tell her the whole story of their Saturday night in the country. The word dancing was a clue, *dancing*; he knew right away he shouldn't have said that, but Lorca missed it. When they left the restaurant they wandered into a club across the street from the Chantecler and stayed until it closed at three a.m. The young men danced, partied with other people on the terrace, got into some stuff David didn't want to talk about. Tomas drank two bottles of beer and walked around outside, happy enough to sit on a bench across the street, listening to the band from there. It was a wonderful night. Tomas stayed away from the people who were coming and going, who stood around smoking pot in the parking lot, hardly anyone wearing masks. The waitress from the restaurant came over when her shift ended and introduced her friends to Eddie and David. "Your father's out on the sidewalk, you know. He says it's too noisy for him in here."

"My dad's fine. This was all his idea." David touched her hand, maybe they could dance. They went out to the terrace.

Already a pattern had set in. In the year that followed their weekend in the country, Tomas and David both became preoccupied with drugs, and made their scores from Edward, who became a sort of bourgeois dealer. Prices went up. Tomas and Eddie became friendly enough that David was no longer needed to act as the middleman. Father and son each made their own purchases. Tomas stayed with LSD, his poison of choice, but David had already moved on to cocaine with the waitress that first night in the country. Sometimes their paths crossed at Eddie's condo, and the three of them would hang around for a while, but for the most part Tomas kept to himself, so he didn't realize that David's drug use had blossomed. David was travelling, spending more time in Ottawa, involved with the fraud case against Rob Barton, the would-be water-treatment magnate, and one night in a hotel bar he met the man's girlfriend, Valerie Wilson. More cocaine. He liked to be busy, in the action. None of that can go on secretly for very long; Lorca began to react, to nag, drawing in her breath. "Where are you tonight, David? Are you coming home?"

For Tomas it went on almost a year. All through the

fall and another particularly icy winter, and then across the spring, Tomas Heyerdahl had his head in the clouds, a strange sort of psychedelic solitude. He'd ride a bus or the metro somewhere and see what happened. He liked movie theatres. He was sure he was never in danger. He never went psychotic or wanted to fly off a balcony, and what hallucinations he had were pretty entertaining. He'd ask himself afterwards, *Did that really happen?* He felt that he could turn it off when he wanted to, waking himself from a dream. He liked to go where there were other people, shopping centres, museums, skating rinks. In the evenings, he'd sit at home. He lived in a three-room condo, though he had divided one room in half as a dark room. The smaller half had the window and a row of cabinets, drawers full of photographs and two drawers of black notebooks. The drug changed everything for him; delight and surprise were his common companions. LSD did not bring him spiritual enlightenment. It made him more observant, which he enjoyed, and he was enjoying his days more, which made him more enjoyable to be around.

One evening in the kitchen, Lorca looked at her father-in-law knowingly. He was sitting on a stool and she touched the back of his head as she walked by. "Charlie saw you downtown yesterday, but you didn't notice him."

"He called to you," she added, "but he felt that you looked right through him." She shrugged, raised her eyebrows. "People talk."

"I'm sorry." Then he nodded. "I'm fine. The thing is, I don't really care about things so much anymore. I'm numb and I want to get over that." He felt a little embarrassed, apologetic. "My mind isn't as fidgety as it used to be. That's a good thing."

A minute went by. "I don't know why people aren't just angry all the time. It's remarkable." She touched him again, Lorca who had a deep well of anger growing inside her. She called Charlie.

Tomas spent Christmas with them, which was wonderful, but he was on his own for New Year's. It turns out even Blue Cheer can't sweep a lonely person through New Year's Eve.

He did run into Charlie and realize it twice during his year of living wondrously. Once, in November, when he was stoned, and another time in March, when he wasn't.

In November they ran into each other and decided to go bowling, and in March they were in Old Montreal. Tomas invited Charlie to come home and they spent the afternoon together at the condo. Tomas had boxes of photographs and notebooks on the dinner table and on the floor around a coffee table, and Tomas pulled out envelopes of pictures to show Charlie. Pictures of his grandmother and the motorcycles, Drolet Street, a picture of his grandmother and his father as a boy in a red Christmas sweater, big white reindeer, the two of them standing up from a table, his father's sleepy eyes, a picture of his grandmother and him. Charlie asked to keep that picture and another one of Tomas and Marie when they were young. The motorcycles fascinated him. "You were so cool," he said, the wheels turning in his head, *This is what my family is like too.*

Tomas showed him the darkroom, "I don't use it anymore but you could if you'd like to. I'll teach you." Charlie was interested but he didn't need it; it was from another time. What he needed was a better computer. Tomas steered the conversation toward school. He talked about cultural geography, anthropology. *People, man.*

No one ever knew that they'd met. They never saw each other alone outside those two times. Charlie didn't come back to use the darkroom, but when Tomas visited the house Charlie showed him photographs. There weren't any pictures of Tomas where he or Charlie shouldn't have been.

The bees spent the winter in hibernation too, and in the spring Lorca and thousands of bees came out again, clean and beautiful, wooden hives, new trays, up onto roofs around the city with two new locations near Lafontaine Park. Paradise. She called Tomas to invite him over for dinner. It was rare for them to be alone together. David wouldn't be home until late. Tomas sat at the counter while she cooked. "Tomas, this is too hard for me. You have to stop taking drugs."

He nodded his head. "Yes, all right." She was serious, today was the day for her, and she looked at him with the question in her eyes until he said yes again. "Clear enough."

"Thank you." She felt good. *But that's the easy one.*

○

Studies have shown that people who win large sums of money in a lottery generally spend it all within five years. W*hoosh*, it's gone, and then they find themselves in real trouble; broke, unemployed, usually addicted to at least one thrilling substance, and no one to call them *my sweet honeybee*.

Lorca's life had changed in a strange, invisible, and fundamental way. In the first few weeks after winning the lottery there were not many hours when she was able to just forget about the ticket. During the first week especially, the news reported that the winning ticket had been purchased in Montreal, and then they reported which convenience store the ticket had been purchased at, with a picture of the store owner, and it was the store on the corner where Lorca and her family lived and stopped in a few times a week, for milk, for whatever. It was the talk of the neighbourhood. And then the fact that no one had claimed the prize became another news story, another topic of conversation for quite a while, especially on social media. People reminded each other to check their wallets and purses, their hiding places, the pockets of their old jeans. Look under the seats of your car. Don't wash your clothes.

The owner of the store would be eligible for a hefty bonus once the winning ticket was cashed, and he'd have his picture on a poster, which would be good advertising for the store; he'd be given money and a plaque, but only when the prize was awarded. He sat at his counter with a small television running all day, watching golf or something else, anything, a lot of his job was waiting (they also serve who only sit and wait), and trying to figure it out, trying to remember the face of every person who bought lottery tickets. As with most of the neighbours, he and Lorca were on a friendly, no-name relationship, and one day when she was picking up a litre of milk, he smiled and said, "You haven't been buying lottery tickets lately."

It took her by surprise. There, shit, another thing she hadn't thought of. "No. I'm saving my money. I never win anyway." She tried to laugh but she felt awkward. "What the hell, maybe I'll win this time," she said, and bought a ticket. She would have to be more careful. She bought tickets every week after that, just as in the past, but when she had a chance she left the tickets under a pebble on the bench where the local alcoholics spent their afternoons. She liked the idea of them winning millions of dollars; that would be interesting to see. She thought of burning her own winning ticket, or giving it away anonymously (though it already had her signature on the back). Could she do that to David and Charlie, burn twenty-three million dollars? Would they be able to forgive her if they ever found out? Months flew by. More and more now she forgot about the lottery ticket, and she was surprised sometimes to come across it stuffed into her wallet behind old grocery receipts or a twenty-dollar bill. She lived out her decision without ever putting it into words.

Travelling Exhibit

"Can you fly a plane?"

"No."

William Munk is crossing the border into New York State. The Adirondack Mountains await, he opens his palm as though at a great vista. The plan was to veer west to Syracuse and Buffalo. Go over the head of Pennsylvania and drive by Erie, PA. He would spend an hour or so in Pennsylvania, the I-80 along the lake, and then on into Ohio. Stay in some motel around Cleveland, which he expected to be his first real stop. See the Rock & Roll Hall of Fame. And then right into downtown Chicago, spend a day or two there. Look for Muddy Waters, Frank Lloyd Wright. All in all, Munk had to cover about three thousand miles across the US. The speed limit in New York State is 65 mph—ergo, forty-six hours. In Pennsylvania and Ohio the limit is seventy; forty-three hours.

The border guard just stares at him for a minute as though he can see in Munk's eyes whether he is lying about flying an airplane or not. He's sure he's lying. They just look at each other, the window is down, but Munk doesn't stare, and he doesn't squirm. The guard has Ray Bans tipped up on the top of his head. The guard says nothing and Munk knows enough not to speak. Just wait. Be plain. Try to attract as little interest as he can.

"You're sure you can't fly a plane?"

"I'm sure, yes. I'm a carpenter. Why are you asking me that?"

The guard nods, weary with all these shady people coming by him every day. "Pull your truck into bay number three"—he indicates the end of the building with his chin— "around the corner." The guard holds Munk's passport, driver's licence, and the letter from Tomas in his hands. "Wait over there," he says. "I'll be with you in a few minutes." The guard walks away.

Munk drives into the spot and gets out of the truck. No one else is being pulled aside like this, and now he's getting nervous. He sits on a bench. What's this shit about a plane? If the guard decided to search the truck it will take hours, and the guard will just get more and more pissed off, and Munk will be pissed too. He's thinking about the mess in the truck, and he's thinking of the photographs. There are twenty-eight pictures and eight of them are nude photos of Marie. One of them is six feet high. What's the guard going to think about that? He had explained to the guard that he was just going to Vancouver. "I want to drive across the US to Seattle because it will be faster. I'll drive up to Vancouver from Seattle when I get there."

"Why are you doing that?" the guard asked.

Munk unfolded Tomas's letter explaining that Munk had been hired to deliver the photographs to Vancouver for an exhibition. The letter included dates of the exhibition and the gallery's complete address and phone number.

The guard reads the letter, taking his time. Munk feels he's milking it now, jerking him around. He breathes deeply. He has one hand on the window ledge. The fucker's as tall as Munk is sitting in the truck.

"Do you have drugs in the van?"

"No sir."

"Do you yourself take drugs?"

"No sir."

"Never?"

"Never."

And that's when he asks, *Can you fly a plane?*

He walks into the office. Munk thinks to call the gallery, but it is only eight o'clock in the morning in Vancouver and the gallery doesn't open until noon. The guard comes back outside. "Are you a carpenter or a delivery man?"

"Both, I guess. Tomas is my friend and I wanted to take this trip anyway. I've never been out west."

"Why didn't your friend bring the pictures himself? Or why aren't you with him?"

"He drives a motorcycle. He's driving across Canada on a motorcycle and I'll meet him there." Munk just leaves Marie out of it. Simplify. "He's going over Lake Superior. Staying in Canada, which is what I should have done."

The guard frowns, he squeezes his lips together and screws up his face like something smells. Maybe he's deciding how flaky this all is. "I do a lot of work for the Montreal Opera Company," Munk tells him. "They'll be open now and they'll tell you who I am."

The guard lifts his chin, enjoying himself. "You an opera singer too?"

"What? No. I'm a carpenter. I build stage sets."

The guard is getting bigger or Munk is getting smaller. It's his fucking authority, all that shit around him. The badge.

"Open the back door."

Munk sighs. *Here we go*.

"Wait here," the guard says, "I'll be back." He turns to walk inside again.

"You're really scaring me," Munk calls after him. "It feels like I'm going to wind up in jail just because you don't like me.'"

The guard stops and smiles at that, he shrugs, "I have nothing against you. But I don't like that truck. Just wait there."

Munk waits on the bench again, a long time. He can count four cameras around him, he's being watched. No one pulls into bays one or two. Finally, the guard comes back out. "All right, let's have a look-see."

"This is freaking me out," Munk says. "Can I just forget about it and go back to Canada? I'll just go the long way around Lake Superior."

The guard stares at him for a long time, like he can see into his soul. Munk is waiting for him to ask about flying

122

the plane again, but he just sort of laughs and says no. "We're into it now, little buddy."

Munk is thinking of the photographs. There are twenty-eight photos, and each one is crated separately. Munk and Tomas built a slotted structure into the van, two by fours and plywood, so that each crate can be bolted into its own slot, vertically. None of the pictures moves or touches any other. He's trying to remember which image is where. He slides one of the smaller crates out of its slot. The guard is standing beside him and Munk unscrews the clamps and opens the top of the crate, doing it slowly, trying to stretch the time out, trying to make the process seem like more of a problem than it actually is. Really, he's trying to bore the guard. And he's hoping he's not wrong about the pictures, that he won't open one of the nudes. But it's the photo of the skinny man standing on the street dressed in an old tweed jacket with a string tie.

The two of them stand there for a while, Munk and the border guard, looking at the photograph, and the guard finally clears his throat. "That's pretty good. I like the colour." He reaches up and pulls on another, larger crate, and they slide it out together. The guard is taking over and Munk can't control what he sees. He tells himself, fuck it. He'll take whatever happens now, get it over with. He opens the crate and there is Marie all in her glory in the shadows of the bedroom. The guard doesn't comment, but he likes it and he chooses another.

One of the other guards comes out to help and they tell Munk to sit on the bench. The two of them pull out all twenty-eight photographs. They're having a great time. The photographs are either leaning against the truck or propped up along the walls, and the crates are open on the ground all around them. There is a six-foot colour photograph of Marie standing naked near a window, and they keep turning back to that one. She's holding her arms behind her. It's a great picture, one arm is bent at the elbow and she's holding the other arm in her hand. A very simple, striking photograph. But it's huge, as big as they are. You can feel Marie looking back at you. Munk just does what he is told, saying as little as possible, but when they're all looking at that picture he speaks up. "It's just realism. You know? It's not pornography." By then he knows he's screwed and he's wondering if he'll just be refused entry and sent back to Canada, or if the guard will confiscate all the pictures.

And then a third guard comes out of the building and the three of them stand together, looking at the photographs and talking in low but excited voices, nattering, something's going on. Then Munk's guard walks back to him and raises his hand. "It's fine," he says. "Go ahead." He gives Munk the papers and the guards go back into their office.

Just like that, it's over. What the fuck? What about the airplane? He packs the pictures back into their crates and puts them into the truck. Brother, he can't get out of there fast enough.

So there, that was the first exhibition of Tomas's photographs, to a somewhat hostile audience. No sales.

He pulls off the highway at the first exit and finds a restaurant, stops for coffee and asks where to buy liquor.

Forty-five minutes later he's back on the road with two bottles of Jack Daniels tucked behind his seat, and he's trying to get as far away from there as he can, as fast as he can. He wishes he'd never crossed into the US. He'll be stopped by a state trooper and end up in some cowboy jail, or they won't let him back across the border into Canada. He is filled with anxiety.

An hour or so later Munk pulls into a restaurant on Route 88, asks for a lot of change and then leaves a message on Tomas and Marie's answering machine, which they only hear when they return home five weeks later. He tells the whole border story. "The fucking guards," he says. "Now they're never going to let me back into Canada."

And that is the end of the Munk. He never shows up in Vancouver. About a year later Tomas receives a phone call from a café in Ann Arbor, Michigan. The café is named My Cubist Grandfather's Nap, right on the edge of the university campus, and they like to show artwork by mostly local artists on their walls, offering the pieces for sale. Munk left two of the photographs there with Tomas's name and telephone number. They were priced at eighty dollars each. The manager of the café wondered if Tomas would like to come and get them, it was time to take them off the walls.

"No, thank you. Please just give them to someone if there's anyone who would like to have them."

"They're good frames," the manager says.

Another photograph turns up in Roswell, New Mexico, almost two years after that. A woman bought a photograph of Marie on a hardwood floor at a garage sale for two dollars. Tomas's name and number were on the back, and the woman decided to call. "I like the picture a lot."

"Thank you," Tomas says. "I'm glad. It's a picture of my wife."

"Oh," she said. "Well, now I like it even more. How did it get here all the way from Canada?"

Eight years after that, Munk sends a letter on blue airmail paper from an ashram high in the Himalayas in Northern India. He apologizes, and tells the whole story again in great detail. He feels very guilty about that peculiar time in his life, and he hopes that Tomas can forgive him. He says he's living in the ashram now with a guru who can be in two places at once, among many amazing things. The man can bend a spoon with his mind, Munk has seen it with his own eyes. The guru is always laughing, "But he doesn't like to do these things," Munk writes, "frivolous entertainments, but sometimes people need visual aids to help us believe."

Marie and Tomas are sitting on the couch. Tomas holds the letter in his hand. "Still, it must be hard for the guru not to show off now and then. I think I would."

"I'll get a spoon!"

Tomas doesn't think to answer Munk's letter until almost two years afterward, and they never hear from him again.

A Honeymoon Waltz

The lithesome bikers stayed off the highway and found their way through a line of small roads, from here to there, mostly gravel or dirt, that somehow wound together into a kind of path that is not on any map you can buy. At times they had to stop to think it over. *We could never find our way back.* East? West? West of what? They zigzagged like that along Lake Superior, just trying to keep the feel of water on their left. By noon they hadn't gone far at all, but they did come across a small hotel with a grassy beach among the rocks. They parked the bikes and stopped to eat, rented a room with a view over the lake, and that was that. Done for another day. "You do realize that we're never going to get there."

Tomas made light of it. "We'll catch up." Of course, he didn't know his photographs were on their way out into the ether, scattering, sayonara exhibit, crated up in a carpenter's dirty blue truck.

"I'm looking forward to a bath."

In the evening Marie made a list: pictures of men

standing in the water backing a motorboat into the lake, close-ups of rocks, grass, trees, insects, a very pretty weed called flowering rush, the landscape out over the lake, two people in a canoe, and the line where the water comes up against the shore. A few touristy pictures, the Three Pines Inn—their home that evening. A picture of the room. Three postcards of Tom Thomson paintings. "I thought they were more stylized than they are. Actually, he painted what he saw."

There was a photograph of Marie pulling a sheet away from her, inviting him in. Tomas photographed what he liked to see.

They were with each other all the time, all the time. "What are you doing now?" Pictures of Marie with a book on the towel beside her. Pictures of Tomas or Marie climbing across rocks, small boulders, climbing away from the hotel. Clambering like spiders, though somewhat less graceful.

The day was hot but the lake was cold when they first waded in, trying to shrink their bodies into the water. "Come on, you have to just dive in." All the photographs are for later, of course, some other time he will print such pictures of her beauty, and he will marvel at the lines of her face, her cheekbones, and how much of her there is in her eyes, her shoulders magnificent in a sleeveless shirt, her unguarded smile. That will be some future evening. But here he lives in the present, he lives within her. It can be a wonderful thing to find you have taken root in the path of another person's life and grown there.

Marie swam underwater and then came up to the

surface just in front of Tomas. She brushed her hair back with her fingers and then she moved into his reach, the water deep enough for privacy, her hands on his shoulders, he was holding her waist. There were a few other people on the beach but they gave themselves this moment as though no one was around. He licked the water from her shoulder and kissed the softness of her neck. His hand slipped under her bikini to her nipple. She brought her lips to his and then she floated back away. She was laughing. "It's embarrassing!" She dipped her face into the water, covering her mouth and nose, and then turned up for air, coming forward through the water like a child's version of a preying fish, wrapping her arms around his neck again. There was a dog on the grass, people walking around, though they stayed closer to the small beach than to the rocks where the bikers had come into the water. There were two people fishing from a rowboat.

They rented a red canoe and went out on the lake. They spread out hotel towels on the grass in the sun. In the pictures from that day, you can see her skin tanning from one to the next, but Tomas was just burning redder.

The Northern Pines Inn was right on the shore of the lake, twenty metres from the water, a big, three-storey wooden house that had been renovated and turned into a hotel, wooden walls with a stone fireplace, overstuffed furniture, long low chairs, and four couches, cushions with moose motifs. Other animal decorations adorned shelves and tables. There were reproductions of Group of Seven paintings on the walls. Tomas and Marie had been given a room that looked out over the water. They ate on the deck of the hotel, and then she took a bath, lounging and lazy, soapy skin. At ten o'clock at night she was sitting at a wicker table by the wide-open window. She could see the lake straight ahead, the moon in a starry sky, she could smell the water. *We are in the Northern Pines Inn on Lake Superior. I feel I can almost touch the lake from the window of our room. We swam and ate like vacationers and we are already a day behind.* It was early when they took their arms and legs to bed but after midnight that they fell asleep.

Marie turned in her sleep, which woke Tomas. He laid on his back and looked up at the ceiling. He slid out of the creaky bed, put on some clothes and walked down the hall. When he returned to the room, Marie was awake. "What time is it?" She sat up in bed and looked out the window. The view to the left was thick with trees, fir trees and ash. They could hear someone sweeping the big deck downstairs, moving chairs around. "Let's go outside." City people. The morning was cold and damp, waiting for the sun to burn off the dew. She was wearing her jacket with the soaring hawk, looking very urban at the Northern Pines.

"We'll make up some time today." And they rode all the way to the end of Manitoba, so fast that afterwards they would hardly say they'd been there. They passed two blue Porsches that seemed to be travelling together. They passed them cautiously, first one then the other, step by step, without incident. They saw a few truck stops. They drove too many kilometres in one day.

○

The silver Porsche is parked under a streetlight in a lot off 17th Street in Calgary, Alberta. The driver is about a block away, in a bar called The Great Speckled Bird, talking to a girl who is a management student at the University of Calgary. Her name is Heather Carlyle and she is a very attractive girl, tall and willowy, with long blond hair the colour of fresh corn, almost to her waist, and a wide, provocative smile, smooth skin. Her face is perfect, almost featureless. She is the most beautiful woman in the room by far. She has an unusually soft voice, as though she's whispering. She came here with friends but she is standing at the bar alone with the Porsche driver now. There are a lot of people in the bar and the music is loud. The driver has to keep leaning closer to hear what she's saying. Her voice is drawing him in. Sometimes he can feel her hair touching his face. He can feel her breath on his skin, and she can feel his breath on her skin. She asks him what he does for a living.

"I'm an actor."

She tilts her head like an inquiring dog, smiles. "Are you a movie star?"

"No, not yet, but I do get work. I've been on a few TV shows and I've just finished a feature film, which will be on television next spring."

"Huh, so I'm hanging in a bar on 17th Street with a movie actor. I will say you are handsome enough to be a movie star. Are you shooting a movie in Calgary?"

"No, but thank you. You're pretty good-looking

yourself." He raises his glass, they both know it's true. "We make a good pair leaning over the bar like this. Someone should make a movie about us. I'm on vacation. I just finished a shoot in Northern Ontario and I have some time off so I'm travelling, getting out of town for a while. I might go to Banff."

Around midnight they leave together, and he is right, they are a good-looking couple walking around to his car, two long-legged specimens, they shine, they reflect light, loose in their limbs, slipping into the low Porsche. He drives to the hotel and Heather spends the night up in the room with him, and they enjoy themselves. In the morning he orders room service. Heather wraps herself in a sheet and walks to the bathroom when breakfast is delivered. He likes the lines of her body in the sheet, the way it accents her figure as she moves, and he likes her bare shoulders. He unwraps her when the waiter leaves. While they are drinking coffee, Heather mentions that her family is in Vancouver. "I was offered a job here in Calgary for the summer," she says, "but they've kept me waiting for weeks. It won't happen now, so I'm going home to Vancouver until next semester."

They are naked, stretching out across the bed, the muscles in his arms and his legs as long and straight as he can make them. They are content. And just in that moment one simple axis of the world clicks into alignment with another, and the playful fellow with the silver Porsche—the car Marie is still looking for everywhere she goes—stretches out on a bed with Heather Carlyle, their long legs and arms entangling, a big bed in a rented room on the twentieth floor. He stretches out inside his karma with his movie star smile.

"Why don't I drive you there?" he says to Heather Carlyle.

She is surprised but she likes the idea. "Yes." She touches his hip, she can dazzle the TV star. "That would be wonderful."

"Where do your parents live? Do they have a big house?" Now he's keen, wondering where is he going. "What do they do?"

"It's a pretty big house, two stories, with an attic room and a basement, and a really nice garden. My mother is a serious gardener. It's the house where I grew up. My father is a financial analyst. He makes a lot of money. My mother has a small art gallery, she specializes in photography."

Plainly for the Camera

Marie stands plainly for the camera. She holds her hands out a little. She thinks about forgetting who she is for a moment, trying to let herself become instinctive. She does enjoy her body when she watches the way he looks at her. This is another part of her life now. She bares her teeth, curls her fingers like claws. She is not wild but pretends to be. She is naked and he is not, the camera is a most important part of his clothing. They move around the room in tandem but apart. They are each moving in their own interest and they speak infrequently. "Are you cold?" He holds the camera high and a little away from his face, watching her and watching her through the lens. Two ways of watching. He moves in relation to her, an influential satellite in jeans with no shirt, bare feet. The camera often covers his face. He crouches, he stands, always in response to her movements. She watches his hands, his thumb, the way he holds the camera. She bends her knees and sits down on the floor. She folds one knee under her and her other leg is almost straight, her knee raised. In the photograph he sees her back, the line of her spine, part of her thigh, she is turning away from the camera, both arms leaning to the floor, out of sight. Her breast is partly visible, seen from an angle, and her hair hangs down over her shoulder: that's his photograph. Years later he will be disappointed because her face is turned away, he can't see her eyes. He will think of the pleasure they had with their bodies, but he can't hear her voice at all in this picture.

Sunday, April 9, 1981. I told Tomas that I would like him not to use my name in the pictures anymore, I am uncomfortable with the series idea, already up to number fourteen. I don't mind at all that he takes the pictures, actually I often enjoy it, and I'm very glad that he wants to, but there is a real disconnect between the person in the pictures and me. At first I used to look at them as though I was looking at myself, but not anymore. In some of the pictures he is separating me from my body. It's a female form put into various physical attitudes. "My body is an object," I said, "so please don't give it my name." Tomas agreed. He understood, but he talked about other pictures. The ones that are almost family pictures that could go in an album, as though they were snapshots that he would describe, This is Marie near the umbrella palm in our living room. Could that be called *Marie Near the Umbrella Palm*? We talked about what the pictures are for. The point seems to come down to who he is showing them to. Private pictures and public pictures; though he said that he is trying to make art, and when he succeeds of course he wants to show it to people, put it up on a wall. He is anxious about the public/private issue, but he has agreed not to use my name. He also said it will be much more difficult now, thinking of me as a construct. *Female Form with Umbrella Palm. Woman in Her Living Room.*

Skies Like This

Coming into Saskatchewan, they exited the Trans-Can-ada again, veering crookedly northward instead of west. Small two-lane roads rolled through fields of grass or fields of wheat that made them think of gold, humming parts of that song, *Heart of Gold*. They had taken the visors off their helmets, light and wind on their faces. Their arms were becoming part of the handlebars. They stretched their fingers, let their left hands lie open in their laps or stretch into the air. They looked like siblings now, white T-shirts and jeans, wind billowing through their shirts. Now and then they passed a farmhouse, some dogs running, barns, bales, and twice a yellow school bus. It was yet another *where are we* sort of day. They passed through a town called Van Huijstee, buildings along both sides of the road, grocery store, gas station, a white wooden church with a graveyard behind it, and a sign pointing to something called the Trombone Oak Museum, twelve kilometres away. A little while later they passed over a small rise, a hill where you could get the idea that you're driving right up into the clear blue sky, and then found themselves coming down a long slope—a slow, gentle angle down, but the descent was about four kilometres long. They could see all the way to the end of prairie earth in every direction, but they were already growing accustomed to that. Far ahead, where the road flattened out again, there was a large dark pool in the field on their left, and as they came up closer to it suddenly hundreds of birds flew into the air all at once with a racket of their wings slapping against each other. For a moment the sky filled thick with birds, a great cloud of birds over their heads, beautiful, wide wingspans, flapping fast in all directions. Tomas and Marie pulled over to the side of the road.

"What was that? Geese? What are those birds?"

"Herons?" The two of them got off their bikes to stand on the side of the road and watch the sky and the fields. "They have legs like herons." There were birds all around them, circling in the sky, or watching them from the fields. They rolled the bikes across the road and pushed them back toward the flooded field. They parked on the shoulder and walked over to the water, where they sat on the side and waited, a camera in Tomas's hands.

"Who is more patient?" Marie asked him, "you or two hundred birds?"

"Me. Always me, if you don't mind." They waited for the birds to come back, quietly. And the birds slowly returned, a few at first, at the other end of the water. The humans sat quietly, they didn't stand up or move around. Marie decided the birds were cranes, and she was right, they were sandhill cranes, with four or five-foot wing-spans. In about forty-five minutes all the birds had settled. Tomas took photos until another roll was finished. Then they sat whispering together for more than an hour, watching the birds with the birds always aware of them, sitting like that and whispering.

In the end it was a yellow school bus rattling down the slope that got the cranes all wired up again. The sky went wild and the school bus was full of children yelling, "Look at that! Look at that!" The cranes squawking in panic.

Tomas and Marie walked back to the road. They drove off quietly but still left the sky full of trumpeting wing-span behind them. They drove for another hour or so, not sure where they were and deciding at crossroads what they should do next. This was choose your own adventure time, looking around. There was more sky than earth to the world there, and small, small objects in between. The sky defined their environment the way blocks of tall buildings do in the city, the sky framed their sense of self. It was blue and cottony, the sun going down, a wide-open world with cumulus. They had the feeling they could go anywhere. They were coming into more grassland now, arrows and distance signs for towns they'd never heard of, and the maps were packed away. They stopped at a family diner called Anne's in the town of Birchard's Shadow, and had supper sitting at the counter with a wall-length mirror in front of them, talking to each other in the mirror and watching everyone else in the room behind them. They had pasta and a green salad, black tea. Chatty people, friendly, asking about the motorcycles, curious about a woman on a motorcycle. "They're figuring you out," Tomas whispered to Marie. They asked about a gas station, a motel.

"A motel?" There were eight other people in the restaurant and they all looked at each other, couldn't agree on where the closest motel was, but it was surely not close. "You can get gas down the street, but there's no motel."

Tomas and Marie rode out of Birchard's Shadow for a while on a road through Saskatchewan farmland, a quiet world. In a while they noticed a dirt path that led off the road and through the fields, a long and more or less straight line. It was a tractor trail, two ruts with grass between them, hard dirt, not quite wide enough for the bikes to fit side by side. They drove along this path slowly, stopping occasionally to look around. They followed the trail, winding with it, seven or eight hundred metres off the road. They could see in every direction, and there was nothing to see, no houses, no structures at all, a few trees standing here and there. About a hundred metres farther there was a clump of poplars, and the land rose slightly behind that. When they reached the trees they turned off the motorcycles, wrapped themselves in silence with a few birds. They walked into the field, looking for a farmhouse or other signs of people, but they seemed to be completely alone. There weren't even telephone poles and wires there.

"This is the spot," Marie said. She was enjoying herself, motorcycles in the poplar bluff. They felt as though they were defined by two boundless surfaces, the earth and the sky.

She reached out to put her hand on Tomas's shoulder, that habitual gesture. They put up their tent near the trees between the earth and the sky. The motorcycles set on either side of the tent, leaning in, lion machines. Tomas lit the Sterno and they had Japanese green tea with chocolate cookies they'd brought from Anne's. When the sun finally set the sky was filled with stars. This was a sky Marie had never seen before, but Tomas had. "In PEI there can be skies like this."

The ocean and the prairie.

City people, lying on their backs on a sleeping bag, trying to identify constellations. Everything has a name, but they could only name a few: the Big Dipper; maybe Orion. The Little Dipper, Ursa Major—the bear—and somewhere nearby, Ursa Minor. They found the North Star but they were losing interest. They turned their attention to each other, and they slowly took their clothes off, unfolding themselves. Marie and Tomas made love in a field near the poplars, she held him on top of her under the big dark night, starry, starry sky, the world prairie sky over his shoulder, overwhelming her, the way people used to do it. Lying in each other's arms, they fell asleep. They didn't notice that the sky was growing even darker.

It was after midnight when the rain came. They scurried into the tent. There was stunning lightning, bolts that seemed to cover hundreds of miles flashing across the sky. Big sky country, with its own big lightning. Thunder cracked the sky so loud it startled them every time, they could feel it in their bodies and in the ground under them. They were lying together with a space open at the front of the tent so they could watch the sky. They felt very small. The rain pounded on their tent and the walls sagged down. The water splashed on their faces through the small opening, but they wanted to watch. "This is going to knock the tent down, I'm sure. Are your cameras safe?"

"Let's go out," Tomas said. These were people who had gardenias growing in boxes on the railing of their balcony. There was an orchid in their kitchen window. "We'll be just as safe as we are in here." He crawled out of the tent and Marie followed. They stood in the rain, naked, soaking themselves, but they couldn't stand still. Moving their feet, their hands, touching each other, holding their wet bodies, they were laughing. Tomas licked the water off her breast, she stepped into his arms, the water cool but nice on their skin, brushing their hair back from their eyes. Squinting. On the wide-open earth with the lightning filling the sky and thunder cracking so loud it was always frightening. Nature was driving them wild, they couldn't handle it. First it scared the shit out of them, then they started moving around feeling like God's creatures, like they'd seen God's face.

God's face flashed right across the sky with light branching out like a tree, like fingers of a long, many-fingered hand. God's voice was booming, and it wasn't far. Tomas started to run along the path and up a small ridge along the path. He slid on his heel down the other side, out of sight. Marie stayed on the trail, her legs muddy up to the knees, squish, she moved to the prickly grass, walking slowly, watching the sky, head up to the rain, counting seconds between lightning and thunder. Neither realized they had separated. Tomas was standing in the grass on the other side of the ridge. He was thinking about what he could say to someone. *I don't know how to describe where I am.* This made him laugh, no camera in his hands when he needs one, and he repeated it out loud, calling to Marie. "I don't know how to describe where I am."

If they'd seen God, this was the playful God. Tomas could see Marie about thirty metres ahead. She was on the ridge, leaning forward toward the ground and flopping her arms back and forth, waving at mosquitoes. Then she came hurrying back in his direction, her feet slipping, making her yelp and laugh, as though she were dancing on her toes. He watched the silhouette of her running, naked, against the night sky, lightning overhead and she was calling his name. "I don't know how to describe where I am!" And then suddenly a bolt of lightning struck the ground near her. Tomas could see the vein of it reach all the way down toward her. The roar was instantaneous, and she fell like she'd been thrown, the way people fall when they're hit by a car. She went down the ridge on her side, and Tomas ran to her, the roar still hovering in the air. She was rolling on the ground in the rain, shouting, holding her left arm. Tomas knelt beside her, already relieved that at least she was conscious. He could speak to her. He touched her shoulders, the hand holding her elbow.

"Be slow," he said. "Is anything broken? Are you able to sit up?" He touched her face as though to wipe the rain away.

"What a fucking idea that was," she said, but she was laughing too, it was hard to believe. "I fell sideways. I landed on my elbow but it seems to be all right." She moved her arm from the shoulder, in obvious pain, back and forth, up, flexing the elbow. "It hurts but it all moves properly. I landed on my elbow and then down. My right foot feels numb."

She was sitting up in the rain. Tomas touched her ribs tenderly. "Here? How's this?" He was panicked but hiding it.

She slid his hand to another spot. "Here." He helped her to her knees, and then to her feet. "I can walk."

She was moving her own hand tenderly over her ribs. "It doesn't seem like anything is broken, but I'll be bruised in the morning."

They walked over the ridge and back to their tent with their arms around each other, slowly. Now they were moving carefully. She was leaning into him and he held her close, a hand over her head as though he might keep the storm away with the back of his hand. They crawled into the tent and he found a towel, then he wrapped her in the sleeping bag to rest. The tent wasn't quite high enough for him to sit up straight, but he sat beside her, leaning back on a bundle. He slid down onto his side to watch her. She slept fitfully, turning often though there was no space to turn, but she did sleep off and on for a few hours. Tomas was filled with dread and his own responsibility to her. *What can I do now?* Could he somehow take this away, lessen it? Now that she was asleep, he felt the depth of his own fear; he knew he would be lost.

In the morning they had tea and spread their clothes out on the bushes and the wheat. They dried fast in the sun.

They could see the burned spot where the lightning had hit the ground, a jagged scorched circle with a pit in the centre, most of a large rock shattered into little pieces and dust. She had been running only a few metres away from there. The ridge where she'd stood was burned black right up to the crest, but she'd been thrown off immediately, sideways. What if it had hit her? What if Marie had died there in a field, naked in the rain in the middle of the night? She held the thought in her body, in her pain and the nervous energy flowing through her. Tomas couldn't stop touching her. Marie had bruises on her ribs and her foot, but she decided that nothing was broken, and she could move freely, though her body was stiff and a little painful.

The bikes wouldn't start right away. They tried a few times, turning the motors over to work the dampness out. They stopped, walked away to come back later, annoyed, there were fucking mosquitoes everywhere, and then the brakes were tight and squealing until they dried out. They drove slowly along the trail to the road, slipping and shooting mud onto their engines and all over themselves, their bags. Tomas looked over to check on her. They found their way back to Birchard's Shadow. "Good morning you two!" It sounded like Anne was singing, glad to see them. Her name was sewn onto her blouse. She had slept better than they had. "How are you? That was some storm."

One after the other, they washed up in the restaurant's bathroom before eating, eggs and hash browns, tomatoes, a bowl of fruit. Anne prepared a few sandwiches for them to take, for later. She worked in this restaurant all day, morning and evening, afternoons off, six days a week. She touched Marie's shoulder, like a blessing. She called everyone dear. "Thank you. You're a saint," Marie said.

Anne laughed. "Oh, yes, don't you know, I walk on snow."

○

They crossed into Alberta and got hit with speeding tickets right away. A cop with shades and a cowboy jaw. No motorcycle chatter for him, no *let me tell you about when I was a boy*. He looked at their licences. "You from Quebec?" Two minutes in and Alberta had already cost them nine hundred bucks.

"Shit." They started the bikes. Tomas looked up at the sky and he saw the Cessna. He shook his fist at the sky and they both laughed. "I should have said I'm from PEI," he said. "I'm a fisherman's son from Tignish."

"I'm Anne of Green Gables."

"We should have mentioned that we're married. I should have said my wife and me. He might have thought we're just normal people." While they were watching, the plane slowly tipped its wing to them. "Nine hundred fucking dollars!"

By noon they were getting on each other's nerves and there was a long space between the bikes. They were two bikers for a while, leaning forward, helmets and visors, Marie with aches and pains, holding around 125, half lost in thought, mostly angry.

This would have been an appropriate time for them to run into the Porsche driver again.

○

It was the pleasure of night that saved them. It was after ten; Calgary. They'd had dinner in a restaurant with old wooden furniture and booths with red faux-leather seats, a curved wooden bar, with a bartender who had an extremely long black beard, groomed and groomed again, and a number of customers with beards just as long, halfway down their chests. All these men looked like lumberjacks or Snow White's giant dwarves. Women were with them, but it was hard to see anyone beyond the beards, they were the most distinguishing feature of the place. The bar was noisy and playful, low light and loud music. The restaurant also had a terrace in the back, where Marie and Tomas sat. They drank wine and ate dinner with condiments on the table, and then walked back to the hotel. They had arrived in Calgary at noon and checked into a Hyatt. They showered and then slept until eight, knocked out, and showered again. They were walking back to the hotel at ten o'clock at night, a warm summer night in Alberta. They were walking on a wide boulevard, a lot of concrete and not much green in this part of Calgary, not many pedestrians either. They walked back to the hotel, sometimes with their arms around each other, or sometimes one's arm around the other, a hand touching an arm or shoulder. Marie's hand in the bend of Tomas's elbow. Maybe from a passing car they heard Bill Withers singing *Lean on Me*, or maybe it just turned up in Tomas's head and he hummed it a little while they were walking. They rode the elevator up to their room, walked through the door. Marie stopped, wide awake. "Let's just go," she said. "Drive."

About eleven-thirty they were packed behind the hotel. The bikes' rumbling rhythm, ready to go. "We're just going to drive," Marie said.

There was a boy looking out a hotel window, his parents asleep behind him. The dark of night was thrilling. The boy stood between a curtain and the glass, watching Marie and Tomas move around in the parking lot. Night magic. They were moving at the edge of a grey pool of light from a high lamp, and their shadows looked thin and long. When they pulled on their helmets the boy imagined he was seeing space aliens. Their shadows looked like they had insect heads. They climbed onto the bikes and with a little hum, they left. At the corner they waited side by side for the light and they gave each bike a shot of gas, one at a time, listening to the engines. The riders found their way out of town and then slipped into the night, motorcycles and speed and the dark of the starry night. There was no one out to slow them down. The bikes were loud and fast and the sound trailed behind them, one long therapeutic yell. The bike in front saw the one behind as a small white spot in the mirror, and, for the follower, the bike in front was a red light ahead. Their friend in the Cessna watched the lights moving very fast across the night. There were times when that's all he could see down there. He veered away but he did come back to look again, the small lines of light in the dark. He clocked them at 172km but he was only curious. They couldn't hear his plane and they didn't notice him circling around to return to them, he was escorting them into the foothills and then the mountains, waving them out of Alberta, and then he turned back to go home.

How to Shrug

A herd of people come off the metro at Peel station, and a man is waiting for them when they reach the top of the stairs. He is standing between the stairs and the turnstiles. He holds out his arms like a prophet, ready to preach, or he'd just like to stop them as they pass, slow them down at least. He is talking all the while. Charlie can't understand what he is saying, but the man keeps talking, droning on, looking at one person or another in the eye as they go by. No one looks back at him. Charlie is standing to the side, watching. The preacher's clothes are ragged, grey cotton pants, a T-shirt with a picture of a basketball on the front and writing on the back, big red running shoes. There is a white plastic bag hanging from the man's belt, though it seems to be empty. In the crowd a girl is coming up the stairs alone and the man points at her, he speaks directly to her, or at her, and as she is walking by he reaches out and touches her shoulder with one finger, as though pointing her out, choosing her, or as though he is pushing a button on her shoulder. The girl turns her head toward him, annoyed, but then she immediately looks away. Charlie realizes that the man doesn't really want anything, he isn't really even talking to her. She just caught his manic, prophetic attention. He touched her shoulder but he is talking into the air. Maybe he is speaking to himself about her. Maybe not. The girl walks on through the turnstiles, and when she's through there she shrugs the hood of her sweatshirt over her head, barely even using a hand, which Charlie finds so cool. How did she do that? At home later he practises shrugging in a mirror.

I am the Earth
the Plants Grow Through

Monday, March 2,1978. Tomas does not see himself as being poor, he calls it having no money, and he says there is no appreciable difference between having money and not having money, as long as you have enough money to get by, however much or little that seems to be. Money is a consideration in planning your days, not a way to measure them. He has lived years without caring about money. Of course, he means in ·the sense of a person's character, *assholes are assholes*, he says, which is just changing the subject. But he handles money like a poor person. He must learn to think differently. Life is more expansive than he lives it. Tomas never imagines the future, thinking of bigger expenses, that we could take a trip or buy a car or just keep money for the future. That we might have a child. When he gets a cheque we go out to dinner. He brings home flowers. In a sense, it seems that he does not feel himself as living in the whole world, but only our small habitual loop, only today or only this one week. As though it will always be the same, just so simple, and he would be happy with that.

Bertolt Brecht wrote, *the system is founded on the matter of means: anyone without money is guilty*, but Tomas would just laugh at that. He once told me that panic attacks are for rich people; "the rest of us just have a drink." He'd tell Brecht that anyone with money is guilty. I think Brecht would probably agree, though he was rather wealthy himself.

Wednesday, October 4, 1978. "You are upstairs. I don't know what you are doing but you're remarkably quiet. We will talk later. I want to tell you there are ways that I recognize that I am far behind you on the curve of civilization, I know this."

Tomas had left a note on the table under her diary. He'd been having a hard day, his note said. "And by the way, there are other people ahead of me too on the curve, though not so many. I am learning as I go and I am a late learner. There are times when I forget this and that makes my life more difficult. I get the idea that I'm a better person than I am. Then, once in a while, I see it in someone's eyes while we're talking, the way they look at me, or there's something someone says that gets to me, and then I come home ashamed of myself. But sometimes this happens when I'm already at home."

She didn't read the note until later, and then she had to wait, replying to it in her mind, until he came home. She shook her head slightly, apologetic, she put both her hands on his chest and spoke in a low, soft voice, still a bit surprised, addressing it out loud now. "Please listen to me." Later she glued the note into her diary. Something to remember.

It was Marie who bought the little house on Drolet. One grey stone house in a row of grey stone houses, fieldstone, built a hundred years ago, all of them pretty much the same on both sides of the street, row houses from a century past, simple homes, all with the door right on the sidewalk, one step up, no porch, but a little balcony that hung over the sidewalk on the second floor. People, the neighbours or the mailman, walked underneath. It was two-storey house right across the street from a small children's playground, the unofficial Nanette Workman Park, someone's rock and roll cloud. Only a few minutes' walk to Marie's garage. Tomas bought dishes, cutlery, a big plain bed with fine linen and a duvet. I say he bought it, but of course they bought these things; this is what he paid for, but they chose everything together. They bought whatever a house would need in the first few months, Tomas learning to share some pleasant, domestic thoughts. A vacuum cleaner. Soft green tea towels. Two Persian carpets, candles, wine, flowers, a broom and a mop and a pail. A little table with a marble top and a bowl made of glass by the door for their keys. Hooks for their coats, a tray for their boots. In the winter, the windows rattled in their frames. They learned to take walls down, they opened up the ground floor and exposed the stone wall of the dining area and kitchen.

Their first morning in the house, awake too early, they went out walking together. It was so early that the streets were still deserted, though they wouldn't be for very long. The night before the neighbours had already been talking about the motorcycle parked by the sidewalk, worried about noise, someone remarking, *it's a woman who drives that.* Then a block of taller red brick triplexes with outdoor metal staircases, and soon Mont-Royal Avenue. The dawn slowly brightened the city around them. They could hear some traffic nearby. *The ghosts are on their way home now, don't you think?*

"The ghosts meet in the park at night. Some nights we will hear the swings squeaking."

"They lounge in the dark under the staircases."

"Smoking dope."

"You should have brought your ghostly camera."

They were looking for somewhere to buy coffee, croissants or a loaf of fresh, hot bread. Someone must be open early. Where did the taxi drivers go?

Thursday, March 17, 1983. Saint Patrick's Day. The parade was last Sunday but the party spirit lives on in the bars. We all wore something green today though we are not Irish. They say that everyone's Irish today, but in reality it's just a good excuse to get drunk. Tomas has gone out for the evening with his camera, but he will stop to meet up with his friend, Michael C., at some point, and will be home pretty late. David is sleeping. He had a busy day with a party and brought home two little muffins with sloppy green icing for our dessert. This leaves me alone in the quiet to collect myself this evening. Truthfully, I like this very much. Sometimes this is the best I can do. To go over the events of my life in my own perspective, slow as a salamander. What I see and what I understand. A solitary woman with a cup of tea, green tea of course. These notebooks are a kind of base for my life, my private corner and my private language. Lucky it's so portable, but when I read over the past it has kind of dream logic to me—I see what I've included and what I have left out. It's interesting how much I do seem to remember of what has been left out.

Later in life it will sometimes seem to Marie that she's lived two lives—the one that she knows in her memory, the one that she tells when she thinks of something that happened, an anecdote, or maybe a troubling memory she can see in flashes when she's lying awake at two in the morning; and the other life, in much more detail and such slow rhythm, which is written in her diaries. She writes in the notebooks in her present, just one evening—moving day, for example, with Tomas listening to music at the other end of the room, cardboard boxes everywhere—but when she reads in the future does she think it will it be a way of living in the present again? Do people often read their diaries over?

"Who is the reader?" Tomas asked her. "Would you like me to read them?" She would not, and he never did, until many years later. But he did ask about the diaries every now and then; Marie would be closing the book, or picking it up, carrying it to a table, "Are you writing to yourself now, or yourself in a few months, or years in the future?" And then he'd come back to it months later, inquisitive, working it out again in his own mind.

"Is it that you would like to suggest ideas and thoughts to your future self?" Would she like to question her future self? Is she questioning herself now?

"It's a record, and it's a thinking tool, a way to keep focus, and I do read them over sometimes to check on how I've been doing. How's my grip on reality? Often it's just events, this happened and that happened, which is useful, but it can be an examination of conscience too, and my understanding grows in writing it down, with the attention and organization of events in my present life. We are attentive to our own lives. No?"

"Yes, of course." In Tomas' mind it was similar to the process of printing photographs, darkroom work, focus. Concentration, bringing out an image.

They were sitting in the living room, near each other, David was asleep upstairs. They had music playing low, a guitar player with an oboe and bass. It was a quiet, tired night. She had the book in her hands and a floor lamp over her shoulder.

"Imagine all the days that leave no trace, ignored."

A picture conveys the emotion, rather than the world the emotion then lived within.

We do not remember days, Cesare Pavese wrote, *we remember moments.*

"In the future you will find old photographs that you forgot about in a drawer and we'll only sort of know what we're looking at, we will recognize the person or remember the event, but we'll be making up most of what we see, the life the photograph documents. It'll be like looking in a convex mirror, the image will just offer a suggestion."

She opened the book and read an entry to him, a few pages about a day, mentioning David and Tomas. He enjoyed hearing it, he relived that day, and when Marie finished he thanked her. He was touched. "Anyway," she said, "I don't know that these notebooks will even exist for me to read in the future, in thirty years? How can I know that? It's hard to imagine."

"It's possible that someone in the future will come to know you only by what you've written in your diaries."

"Will they know you only by the photographs you have taken? What will that tell them?"

"They'll be impressed with all the pictures I've taken of you. They'll know me that way. They'll say, look, this guy was obsessed." Marie laughs in the way that always makes him happy. He would tell the future. *There, see.* But seriously—seriously—how to photograph that laughter?

In the future, Tomas will have an intricate model train set and a stoop in his stance, a bend in the shoulders. He will no longer have Marie to take him in hand, take him in her arms as though to straighten his posture like a bent stalk, stand up straight, Tomas, now you will have to exaggerate even until it feels unnatural. There will be a dream where she comes to him in the old Volkswagen. He doesn't see her face but he knows it is Marie driving their car. The door is open, he looks down at the floor on the passenger side, he looks at the old seat, but so far in his dream he does not climb in to sit down. His dreams are filled with shared objects that are signs of her. It seems curious that he never looks up in the dream, never looks at her face. Why is that? He would like to very much. Marie's substance now is in the bridge between them, her substance is made of her diaries and his dreams.

He will live in a basement but his apartment will be at the front corner, and so he will have windows on two sides, the front lawn and the driveway. The front faces east and so he will have morning sunlight. The train set will wind through two rooms, there will be a village, and the tracks will climb and then ride the walls like a mountainside, a cliff, on frames, trestles that he's made from balsa wood, they will cross diagonally at the top of the doorframe. He will sometimes have visitors and a few of his guests will have to bend their heads to walk under it. Tomas will offer a cup of tea.

At the end of the summer, that future summer, Tomas has been reading his wife's diaries once again. It's something he has done before, the first time was a few years ago, a way of invoking her. He has refused so far to share the books with David. There are 193 black notebooks, all out of the dresser drawer, spread around the condo. These days he has no other interests. It is a strange feeling to be reading into Marie's thoughts. He is living with her again, following her cursive hand, sometimes even a note is folded in, his own blockish scrawl. Papers are folded into the pages, David's drawings, ticket stubs, pictures, sketches. It helps him remember the days of their lives together, but he also can see another version of Marie's life, her own personal version. There are long stretches in her diaries when his name doesn't even come up, sometimes he sees himself only in the word *we*. He reads about the issues of her life, concerns he was only superficially aware of, her work, her colleagues. He follows the threads of her curiosity and generative energies through the years. At the same time, he is reading her version of his life, how she thought of him.

On a Wednesday night in September, many years after the diaries were written, Tomas is reading his young wife's diary in bed before he falls asleep. She may have even written some of these entries with him beside her in their bed, she wrote the days he is reading now, or at the dining room table or her desk, or in the armchair with the tall palm and the yellow lamp. Tomas puts her black notebook on the table beside him, turns out the light, and lies down. He still feels Marie with him, her voice, which was speaking from the diaries, is inside him, and he says out loud, *Good night dear*. This amuses him, and he curls into a sleeping position, *goodnight my body*. He imagines Marie answering him, *Good night*, she says, and for a minute he can feel that she is physically there in the bed with him. As he turns around, there she'll be, he could touch her. She can touch him.

Marie once suggested—it was on a Sunday afternoon

when they were visiting her aunt Agnes in a senior's residence—that women are much better at living without men than men are without women. "Look around us," she said. They were sitting in a room full of widows, sitting down to five o'clock dinner, a room full of white-haired ladies in proper dresses, chatter across the room, a waiter served small round glasses of red or white wine, *Roast or salmon today, ladies.* Table after table of women, but there were only a few men in the room, four or five of them wearing jackets and ties in fading shades of brown or blue, and the men were all sitting at tables away from each other, five women and one man, here and there.

Tomas looked around the room. "Well, I don't know whether that's true, but men do seem to die earlier."

"Yes, I guess we do have more practice," she said. She asked Aunt Agnes, "Do the men get together later to play poker or watch a football game?" Agnes shrugged. She evidently didn't have much to do with the boys, although she did have a lot of attention for little David.

Before Aunt Agnes moved into the residence, she had been living in a three-story house where she had lived for the last forty years. Big rooms, beautiful mahogany bannisters. She lived with a cat that would disappear for days at a time. She'd stand at the back door, calling. Marie's uncle had died eight years earlier, and Agnes had stayed on in their home, alone inside their life, using only three of the rooms, and the home grew rundown. It needed too much attention, things her husband used to take care of, repairs, paint. She walked to the grocery store, sometimes she met friends. In the last year or so in the house, she had begun to tape sheets of paper onto all the furniture, with the names of her nieces and nephews and friends, outlining who she wanted to give each thing to when she died. But she didn't die, and she eventually agreed to sell the house and move into the residence. She said it was like a hotel. "I'm so tired of eating," she said. A hotel with happy hour.

Sunday, July 9, 1985. Tomas took some good pictures today. He says that he is focusing as much as possible on the skin around people's eyes, the lines and the puffiness. There are some portraits that are quite moving, and he's able to bring out various emotions from the women. He can make them laugh, though David helps a lot with that. Sometimes Tomas just does nothing until the posing stops. In those pictures you can see the wheels turning in the women's eyes. There's a lot to see. Tomas is a patient man, and he doesn't mind taking many pictures to have just a few in the end. He is quite a good photographer and he hears that often enough; he doesn't doubt himself much.

Music was playing in the house on Drolet. Marie held a dress the colour of turmeric against her body and she looked first in the mirror and then looked through the mirror across the room to Tomas. He liked the dress very much, and said so with enthusiasm, but he was more drawn to the shape of her knees and her bare feet. There were already a few other dresses draped over the bed. He was choosing a necktie, and she agreed with his choice. The kettle whistled and he went down to the kitchen.

People are Water

"All I ever wanted was an ordinary life. Why is that so difficult?"

"What's more ordinary than a bad marriage?"

She was livid. Lorca was a homemade bomb. Her anger was explosive and apparently never-ending. She couldn't see David's face, but she could hear the smirk in his voice. Though he did apologize then. "Listen, I'm sorry. I'm sorry. I'm sorry. I'm sorry. I'm sorry. I feel terrible. I'm sorry. There isn't enough language to say how I feel about this, about myself. But we keep talking about it. Every day I keep apologizing, and I'm growing numb. I want to make it up to you." He was getting over his deceit (he said it didn't mean anything, of course, just adventure), but Lorca was not getting over it. She did not let go, a dog with a bone. Anytime, nights, mornings.

At first she had no idea what he was doing, but slowly she did put it together. And when they talked alone, that's all they talked about.

"All I ever wanted was an ordinary life."

Compulsive, she phones him in the middle of the afternoon to erupt again. *We have a son*. She is standing on Sainte-Catherine Street with the phone in her hand, standing close to the buildings, turned with her face to the wall, standing away from the people walking by. She does not know that Charlie is also downtown, standing right across the street, but he is there watching her. She is holding the phone in one hand and her other hand is brushing through her hair, she's pulling at her hair. This causes both of her arms to bend at the elbow and her elbows are high, which seems to close her off even more, she is part of the wall she is facing, closed off from everything around her. She leans her head forward, talking at the wall. Charlie can't hear what she is saying but he can see the emotion in the nervous way that she moves her body. He takes a photograph.

Lorca puts the phone away and begins to walk east in the direction of Union Street. Charlie starts to run. Lorca is calming down, walking along the north side of the street. Charlie is on the south side, running to get far ahead of her but trying to crouch down at the same time so she won't notice him. He'd like to surprise her. He's staying low and near the walls, keeping traffic and people between his mother and himself. He runs for two blocks, weaving in and out of people, turning into storefronts to look back a few times, making sure that she's still coming in the same direction. When he feels he's far enough ahead he crosses the street at a traffic light and begins walking back toward Lorca, *cool*, and when they come near each other he acts as surprised as she is. *What?* He likes the smile on her face.

"Charlie, what are you doing here?" She hugs him. It doesn't matter what he's doing there. They are standing on Sainte-Catherine Street side by side with their arms around each other. He can see that she has been crying but they are both pleased now. "Let's have dinner downtown tonight."

She walks Charlie to a small Italian restaurant on Drummond Street, one step down from the sidewalk. He has never been here before, and today he's going to dinner alone downtown with his mother. They have come here without discussing his day at school for even a moment. It's still early and the restaurant is preparing for later, setting tables, filling the salt and pepper shakers. The waiter waves them to a table at the front, right by the window, a square table with a red and white tablecloth and a small vase of flowers in the middle. He holds Lorca's chair. He knows that people who are passing by will see them and find it inviting.

"May I have a glass of white wine?" Lorca asks. Charlie equivocates and then asks for water. The waiter brings a small green bottle of San Pellegrino and a glass with a twist of lemon and a swizzle stick. He tells them the daily specials. He is an older Italian man and he is very comfortable in his restaurant, gracious and calm. He can see they are mother and son, and he jokes a little with Charlie, which all three of them enjoy. In befriending the son, he wins over the mother. Lorca and Charlie read the menu. They watch people walking by on the sidewalk. They talk about food. Garlic bread. His schoolbag is on the floor but his camera is on the table. He walks farther into the restaurant and takes a picture of his mother sitting at the red and white table with the window behind her. The waiter offers to take a picture of the two of them at the table together. They talk about many things but through the evening Lorca refrains from making enquiries and offering suggestions about how Charlie should live his life. And he does not ask why she was crying. While they are having dessert he sits in the chair beside Lorca and he scrolls through the pictures in his camera with her. Lorca sees a picture of herself talking to the wall, *oh*, and two other pictures of her sitting at the table, with and without Charlie. But never mind, he says, really, he wants to show her a sequence of photos of children.

Charlie has spaghetti with meatballs, garlic bread, and Lorca, fettuccini with oil and garlic, slivers of zucchini and tomato, a glass of wine. She is sitting at the table with Charlie, admiring his bony boy-man wrists, his knuckles, but in another part of her mind she is always thinking of David. Sometimes she feels betrayed, like a teenage girl, and other times like a woman with a boy-man son. These are very different betrayals. "This doesn't have to change our lives," David had said. "Let it not change our lives."

David. Where did his sanity go? What happened to him was that he let himself slip into the delirium of other people with their addictive tics and manipulations. He let himself become two people, and the delirious one pulled him into that other electricity, away from the David he was at home, further and further, until the person he was at home became a persona.

As her husband distanced himself, her son came closer. He is sitting beside her at the table, he touches her forearm. "I went to the Insectarium today," Charlie says. "There was a school group there, first-grade kids with a couple of teachers."

In a few months, David has seemingly just let go of his family, though he denies it now, they fell out of his hands. He also let go of his work. He is the one who is falling. What is missing in him that allowed him to turn away? In future years, he will struggle often with the inadequacy that is blooming in him now. His son will have pictures of his uncomfortable smile.

On the camera screen, Charlie points out a couple of boys. "These two kids," he says. "There's a hall that's just for butterflies at the Insectarium. These kids came into the butterfly room and they freaked out." He is waving his arms around himself to show her. "There are butterflies everywhere in there and the kids acted like they were afraid, they were running around, ducking from butterflies, *Whoa! Look at that one!* They tried to hide under tables and behind the other kids and behind the teachers, with the teachers trying to brush them off, telling them, *Stop it, stop it*, but the teachers were laughing too. *Whoa! Whoa!* It was very funny, these little kids who are afraid of butterflies."

David calls her to say that Charlie isn't home yet. "No, that's all right. He's with me."

o

Thursday, December 29, 1986. Yes, time is a river and the river follows an orbit. This is the season for being struck by the rhythm of the years and all their annual markers, Christmas, New Year's Day, anniversaries. All the parties, all the feasts, so much food it's disturbing to contemplate. We are such omnivores. We eat and eat and eat. My mother served a sixteen-pound turkey on her best china platter, my father sharpening the carving knife; he makes the steel sound like swords. White linen, crystal wine glasses. A very nice day, lots of presents for David. For Tomas and me, the river's current is smooth, we are swimming comfortably. It is the changes in David that are most striking, he shows us how the years have passed. It is less obvious with us, no pencil marks to compare our heights. During these years the adults' changes are mainly within ourselves, our sense of accomplishment, or however it is that we value the passing of time. Where did the year go? Maybe all the busyness with pomp and ceremony for the events protects us from such troubling introspection. We will kiss and toast goodbye to another year, and welcome in the new. The next day we will eat wonderfully but too much, again, and the day after that we'll get back to our daily lives.

Rain on the Coast

That summer set a new record for seasonal rainfall. It rained for eighty-nine days straight, though it was only on day thirty-seven that Tomas and Marie arrived in town, and they left on day forty-two. There was rain at least once at some point every day. Every day! Sometimes for most of the day. They talked about the rain as much as it fell. Barbara, the gallery owner, explained it all with a logical shrug when they had lunch one afternoon. "We're in a rainforest." This made it more acceptable. They bowed their heads to science, but they left town on day forty-two, early, going back to where they came from.

Imagine the motorcycles coming down out of the sky. Cowboy music an earworm in both their heads, the same song, a pedal steel guitar and a man's voice singing, *I've felt the mountain air, man, I've been everywhere*. This song that stood out for them in the restaurant where they ate breakfast in the morning, a theme song for the day, listening to the sound of the man's heavy voice rattling off the names of towns and thinking about the places they'd been lately. The song kept coming back to them as they wound down out of the mountains. They could add their own verses, *I've been miles above the sea, man, my feet still touched the ground.*

Barbara Carlyle stood inside her gallery. "The rain is good for your skin," she told them. The rain was great for rainforest vegetation, a city with lush green gardens. Tomas took photographs of plants with leaves like tongues. But it was not good for motorcycle engines, and generally not at all good for Easterners, who grow more depressed there every day. In a Harley shop off Hastings Street Tomas and Marie found excellent ponchos with the company name, A Duck's Ass.

They were driving down out of the mountains and they could feel that the city was there for them before they saw it. They were rising out of a prolonged trance. The wanderer hours, each of them alone but nearby, were coming to an end. Traffic was thicker now, a lot of trucks, the distance signs now down to two digits. They were already beginning to smell the Pacific Ocean, though Marie wondered if that was even possible, ninety kilometres away. The bikes wove closer to each other now. They felt frisky, successful. At times they could have reached out to touch hands, but they drove fast.

They pulled into the last roadside stop before hitting the city. There were two fast-food restaurants, a gas station, and washrooms. All equally important. They drove the motorcycles as close as they could to the grass at the back of the parking lot, away from the trucks. As always, getting off the bikes was a rickety ritual of bent-kneed sunyatas, more serious now for Marie with her bruised ribs. They took off their jackets and draped them over the handlebars. He walked in first to pee while she stayed outside with their belongings. People looked over at the woman in a T-shirt and jeans standing alone with two loaded-up motorcycles. She spotted a black Porsche in the lot and walked over to stand near it out of curiosity. Tomas was inside. He was trying to wash his hands, but when he put his hands under the automatic faucet, nothing happened. He tried another faucet but there too no water came out. He passed his hands under three faucets, but no water flowed out of any of them. Other men were washing up with no problems, and they were all laughing. Tomas looked at his hands. "What the hell?" The man beside him started the water flowing and then Tomas put his own hands under that faucet. When he returned to Marie he held out his hands and told her the story. "They don't register. My hands have no substance."

"You have the hands of a vampire." She took his hands in her own and shook them. "Did you get anything for lunch? Never mind, I will." She went inside to pee and wash, without incident, and then looked around the restaurants, looking for something acceptable to eat.

They sat on the curb near their bikes. They had salad in clear plastic bowls with little bowls of Caesar dressing inside. It wasn't very good but they were used to that, the road travellers' menu. They also had a big celebratory chocolate bar and they shared a cup of tea.

They bought gas and got back onto the highway. The bikes were loud dogs. The sun was shining then and they were enjoying their day. They had come almost five thousand kilometres and now they were driving into the city nicknamed Lotus Land.

○

There's an old joke people still like to tell: to test the strength of a marriage, paint a house together. But how would you feel about driving five thousand kilometres on motorcycles over a twelve-day period, sleeping in a little green tent under the sometimes starry night? They pulled into the last roadside stop before hitting the city. They stretched off the bikes and laughed at themselves. The loop held.

The loop held them for forty years. They were together for forty years, joined, and there were days that they would pass each other like two motorcycles a hundred metres apart on a mountain road through a forest. Known. Sometimes excited, sometimes a small acknowledgement. When one watched the other while the other was unaware of being watched, what did they see? Extensions of one another, tidal; their lives together were like tides. They had a child. David. They were joined completely.

Illness, when it came, made them desperate and fierce.

○

When they met, Tomas owned almost nothing that most people take as part of normal, day-to-day living. He didn't have a lot of money, and Marie found it interesting that he didn't really care. He felt he had enough. He had a few dishes, cups, kitchen stuff, patio furniture that he bought in an alley. But he did own a lot of cameras and equipment. There were photographs pinned to every wall. He had an old Hasselblad 500C that didn't work, though he wasn't sure why. He'd bought it at a garage sale, and it just sat on a shelf. The camera was made in 1961, a year before NASA sent up the same model to photograph the moon, and he thought that if his could be repaired it might be rather valuable. "I could sell it and buy a couch for us to sit on," he joked with Marie. She told him to buy two pillows. He did buy new cotton sheets, matching plates, wine, a vase. She brought over towels. She left hair pins and cream by his sink, a toothbrush, lavender soap. That's also what love is like. Tomas came home to his apartment late one afternoon—by this time Marie had a key—and he found the Hasselblad in pieces spread out on newspaper covering the glass table. There was a yellow box with a set of small Allen keys and screwdrivers. Marie wasn't there but she'd left a note, *Don't worry. Don't touch. I'll be right back.*

The Machine in the Garden

Barbara Carlyle, the owner of the Vancouver photo gallery, turned out to be older than Marie and Tomas might have imagined, old enough to be their mother. She had a rather austere demeanour, disciplined, and a general air of intelligence. She was also quite witty, with an offhand, wry way of commenting—offhand in a way that suggested she didn't much care whether anyone heard or not. When they first met her she was wearing a black pinstriped suit, with a black blouse open at the neck. She had white hair swept back from her face. Her face was lined, and she was thin, with prominent features.

She was a New Yorker who'd moved to British Columbia thirty years earlier, and lived her life here. She'd been one of the first curators in Canada to open a gallery dedicated solely to photography, the Carlyle Gallery of Contemporary Photography, and the gallery determined her daily life; photography as art and business. In those years there were still people who would argue that photography was not an art form.

Honoré de Balzac believed that our bodies are made up of layers of ghostlike images, an unknown number of skins laid one on top of the other, and that every time someone had a photograph taken one of the layers was peeled from the body, removed by the photograph. Every camera was ethereal, every picture took away another layer until in the end it removed the essence of a person's life.

Diane Arbus once said that taking pictures was like tiptoeing downstairs in the middle of the night and stealing Oreo cookies.

Barbara Carlyle lived in one of those old dowager homes, on a rise in Kitsilano. Three floors with separate rooms in the basement, which is where Tomas and Marie were invited to stay while they were in Vancouver. She lived with her husband, Michael, and one of their daughters, Heather, who was back in town from university. Two other adult children lived elsewhere, one in Toronto, and one in California. Barbara answered the door when Tomas and Marie rang, and welcomed them, surprised at the sight of these dusty people with motorcycles at the curb. "You've driven all this way on motorcycles!" She told them not to leave their bikes on the street. "Just drive around the corner, take the lane, and come up to the back of the house. I'll meet you there."

She could hear them before they came into sight. She opened the gate and they stopped, then drove the bikes in slowly one behind the other with their feet sliding along the ground. She walked behind them, watching the tires and worrying what the bikes were going to do to the garden over the next few days. It was a beautiful, well-tended garden with a stone path that wound around a raised brick circle, like a well, which had been filled in and planted, and then the path went under a trellis. The motorcycles could barely fit. There was a wooden shed near the house and they parked the bikes by a small pile of pipes against the shed wall.

Barbara led them into a basement apartment, two rooms, and left the key on the kitchen counter. "You can have some privacy while you're here, but you are welcome to come upstairs any time you like. We usually have dinner at seven o'clock. Don't ever feel you have to come, but please know that you are completely welcome any time. I'm sure you'll want to explore Vancouver. It's been raining a lot lately, but it's a wonderful city."

Barbara had no news from Munk. "I'm dying to see the photographs," she said. "Are you worried about him? Should we worry?" They expected they'd hear from him tomorrow, they said. Barbara went upstairs. "See you soon. Dinner at seven."

They unpacked the bikes together and brought everything inside, bags on the couch and the floor. Tomas opened up the sleeping bag and hung it outside over one of the motorcycles. He unpacked his equipment in a corner and Marie ran a bath. Barbara had left six bottles of beer in the fridge with a package of swiss cheese and a jar of pickles. There were crackers in a cupboard, coffee, peanut butter. Marie stretched her legs in the hot water with her feet up near the faucet and a bottle of cold beer in her hand. A thick white towel on a stool near her. "Languid like Cleopatra." Tomas leaned in the doorway. "Cheers."

After a little while he climbed into the tub with her, the faucet at his back and her feet on his chest, her sore foot up to his shoulder, his hands on her legs, her arms, leaning forward, holding the bar of soap and a cloth in his hands. He asked about her ribs and she touched them, *better*, all that driving washing away.

Later that evening Barbara told him of a three-hour photo lab in Richmond and he was out there on his bike when it opened at eight a.m., just in case. He dropped off the sixteen rolls of film he'd shot during their trip, and he said he might need to rent a darkroom. There were two men at the counter, but neither had any suggestions. Tomas pointed at the rolls of film. "I don't need prints, just negatives and contact sheets," but they couldn't promise to do it any quicker than three hours. Tomas came back to the basement apartment, slower in heavier traffic now, attentive to where he was going. He drove down Barbara's street and noticed the silver Porsche parked in front of the house. He stopped and looked it over and then went around to the back of the house. It was nine in the morning when he rode through the garden. Marie was reading a newspaper. There was coffee in a steel thermos with two cups and milk and sugar in small white bowls. "Room service!"

At 11:30, they picked up the negatives and contacts in a padded brown envelope and drove to the gallery. Still nothing from Munk. Barbara was calling around, trying to arrange a darkroom. Tomas and Marie drove to the frame shop Barbara used to buy a lot of plain, black metal picture frames in various sizes. They strapped them to the bikes and drove back to the gallery. Again, all just in case. It was almost three o'clock. Barbara was outwardly calm, but starting to wonder. *Where were they?*

○

Here is an old photograph of Marie Lextase as she is standing up from a table on a screened-in porch one summer evening in the mountains. There was an underground stream running by that cottage, very close to the surface, and so the ground around the cottage was always damp, always as though it had recently rained. It made them think of a swamp. Every night the air was filled with fireflies. David was seven years old and he loved those nights, fireflies in the trees, but they could not be properly photographed. In this picture Tomas took David is sitting at the table next to Marie, and her right hand is touching the top of his head as she stands up. This touch is so fluid, commonplace, completely unremarkable; it takes for granted that they are extensions of each other's body. There is a cup on the table in front of David and he is holding playing cards in his small hands and turning toward her movement. When Marie first held David in her arms, Tomas thought to say out loud, "Look what God gave me."

Marie stands up from the wooden table, next to her son and just across the table from Tomas, who has been trying to photograph fireflies. David is turning to her. By their postures it seems she is speaking to him. She turns and puts one hand on the table and one hand touches

David. The gesture could not be simpler. She is probably saying something about bedtime. Imagine that the wooden chair creaks. Sometimes Marie and David put their hands together, palm to palm. She is wearing a watch with a striped band on her left wrist, her hair is loose and hangs a few inches below her shoulders. In the photograph Tomas can see the fine line of the vein under her skin, the skeletal lines in her hand.

○

When they arrived at the gallery, there was an old man across the street, playing an accordion, and they stopped to listen before going in. He had a blue cloth set out neatly on the sidewalk in front of him. He was large, with white hair and a white shirt with red suspenders. He was playing an old French song that Marie knew, she'd heard it in Truffaut's *Stolen Kisses*, a great accordion melody. When people passing by dropped money onto the cloth the coins bounced and rolled away, and some people stopped and picked up their coins to put them down more carefully a second time. The man seemed to find this hilarious and thanked them profusely. Every giving became an event with him. Of course, a few of the givers couldn't be bothered, and the money rolled onto the street, but the accordionist didn't seem to mind. He joked and talked freely with the people who passed him by, whether they gave or not, and whether they replied or not. He called *hello* to Marie and Tomas. They shouted back and Tomas ran across to leave some coins on the cloth. He called to people in cars when they stopped at the traffic light and they chatted with him while they waited. He played the same tune for a long time, so slowly that Marie thought sometimes that he might have forgotten he was playing it.

○

Barbara had arranged for a darkroom from a local photographer named Elizabeth Mortimer-Lamb. She lived in an apartment near Capilano College, and she agreed to let Tomas use the room and equipment for the night, but only after ten o'clock, and it was important that he work quietly. He had to pay for all materials, paper, and chemicals, and she offered to help for a while if he'd like, though he wouldn't.

Inside the gallery Tomas called Montreal again but there was still no word from Munk. Everyone else was fine. Tomas and Marie sat on a couch and went over the contacts with a magnifying glass and two ballpoint pens, red and blue, sheet by sheet: sixteen rolls of 35-mm film, about 575 pictures. He crossed out the ones that he definitely wouldn't use, half of them, right away. The first five minutes are easy, slashing X like a pirate. He had to come out by tomorrow afternoon with about forty pictures and he could only start working at ten o'clock that night. They went through the sheets a second time, *This one or that one?* They were still making quick decisions, trying to cross out more. Marie or Tomas would make a face with their nose or mouth and that was all it took, *bah*, X. Marie would look away and that was enough, X. She favoured pictures that didn't include her, but of course they almost all did. He circled the pictures he felt pretty good about, final choices now. He was already imagining exposures, sizes. They went through them a third time and narrowed it down to about sixty pictures for him to start with. Some were circled twice, which was good. Some had question marks over them. Tomas made three choices silently and those pictures he checked off only in his mind. *Remember that one*. He was getting excited about the project and he had forgotten the work in Munk's truck. "If Munk shows up now I won't use those pictures."

o

Elizabeth Mortimer-Lamb was a young woman who had faintly purple hair with some white in it, pastel colours, the white was vague as fog, although her natural hair colour was dirty blonde. She wore black or red boots with long laces, sometimes with cotton dresses, sometimes chino pants. A cowboy belt. Her interests were artistic and wide. She was educated. Elizabeth took it all in, the whole world around her; she was wiry, fast, sometimes she'd remind people of the Roadrunner, and occasionally they would mistake her for being disorganized in her thinking, or indecisive. She spoke in terms of images and creation, conceptualism but post-minimalist, neo-expressionism, and she took part in many activities in the arts community. She was well liked and had some excellent friends. Some were lovers, and some of those were pretty good too. Her main interest was photography, followed by performance, another way of thinking of the body as object. The skin as the boundary. She was a regular photographer at live art events around town; they could depend on her to be there, to get the pictures. During the day she worked for a medium-sized publishing company, dealing with much of the daily upkeep work, she kept the office clicking. She enjoyed sitting in during editorial meetings, listening in, writing things down in a spiral notebook, and later she would speak privately with the editors, asking questions, offering her thoughts. Some colleagues were more receptive than others. She was young but she was crisp, she learned fast. She did sometimes see her ideas carried forward and this made her feel wonderful, a more important part of the group.

Elizabeth also worked as a volunteer for a local arts magazine, *Corners*, which was the reason that Tomas could only begin his work at ten. Elizabeth was one of the magazine's editors, and its principal photographer, and she had a lot to do herself that night for the magazine's next issue. She offered to help Tomas because she was quite intrigued by his project. The idea of putting together a solo show in one night, starting from contact sheets, working with pictures he hadn't actually studied before, thrilled her. She also liked the idea of staying up all night working. When Elizabeth offered her help, Tomas thanked her but said he liked to work alone in the darkroom. He thanked her again. He asked if she had enough chemicals and paper, and when he arrived he brought two boxes of printing paper with him, 10" x 12" and 16" x 20", along with three rolls of corrugated board. He also brought a few bottles of beer and a large bag of Ripple chips.

There were already people in Vancouver wondering about Munk. He was becoming mythical, the story of his disappearance. It was good publicity for the show, it meant more people would come. The community was lively: if you rang a bell a lot of people would hear it. Elizabeth had many friends, people she knew in school, at work, at the magazine, here and there. They attended most of the openings and other events around town. Elizabeth had exhibited her own photographs in a local bookstore and at a few group shows. One had been at the Carlyle, which was how she'd met Barbara.

Tomas arrived right at ten. "I hope I'm not too early."

"No, come in. Good timing. I finished working about fifteen minutes ago." Elizabeth had a three-room apartment in Capilano. There was a kitchenette, a living/dining room, and a bedroom, which she'd turned into a darkroom. "I sleep on the sofa there," she pointed, "but don't worry, you won't wake me up. Though you could wake me if you need anything. Anyway, I don't go to bed before midnight."

As usual in a photographer's home, there were pictures pinned onto the walls and one of the clusters caught Tomas' eye. "What are these?" A dozen small, unframed black and white photographs, simple surfaces but of great definition, set together on one wall, facing the sofa. "These are very good."

Tomas's praise made her happy; she'd wondered what she could expect from this stranger she'd invited into her home only because he was a photographer. He knew

Barbara. A man with a show. She said thank you quietly; she knew how good the pictures were. "It's a series of photographs of paper bags. I crumpled them up and then smoothed them out to photograph. It was a difficult exercise in focus, my eyes were starting to go wonky. I had to throw a lot of pictures away, but I do like these."

Tomas was impressed. In each photograph the focus was so sharp along one crease, one particular spot, and the rest of the paper seemed to range away; in focus and greyscale, an inch of paper could make an enormous difference.

In the end, Tomas shut himself in the darkroom later than he'd intended, after eleven o'clock. He and Elizabeth talked about cameras, lenses. She had used a tripod for the bag photos, three spotlights, turning away and then coming back to focus sharper and then sharper again. Obsessive. It was the same in the darkroom, a day of testing for each picture. While he worked Tomas would be thinking of these pictures in the back of his mind and it was going to affect his own output, though he didn't need anything to slow him down that night. Elizabeth watched television and spoke on the phone. She made up her bed and tried to read, but she was thinking too much about Tomas in the other room. She fell asleep well after midnight, under the blankets with a book in her hands. She was wearing pyjamas, which she hadn't worn in two years. Tomas came out a few times throughout the night, using the bathroom or getting water, quietly, not even looking toward her. It would have helped if he had earphones, music playing, to keep him awake. In all, he printed thirty-eight photographs. The smallest were only four by four inches, and there were four of those which would fill small slivers of wooden frames. The largest was one photo he had to print on six sheets of sixteen by twenty paper, so almost four feet by four feet. Each sheet would have its own frame. He turned the enlarger to face the wall, projecting the image as large as possible, then pinned sheets of paper onto the wall one by one, exposing parts of the picture in order. He lost definition in making it so large, but still liked the final effect anyway. He talked to himself while he worked, but he didn't know he was doing it, and it wasn't loud enough to bother Elizabeth. He was like a swimmer who has dropped into the pool. He knew the world around him as pictures, every moment had a frame, angle, a suitable depth. Images were like words for him, the sound of people's voices, fluid, instinctive, his own intimate grammar.

The largest photograph was a picture of Marie walking on a path through trees, a wooden bridge with rope railings. She was quite small in the picture. It was a black and white photo of a forest, maple trees and their leaves in a million grey tones, almost silver in places, with a woman walking to the left of centre and down a bit. The eye was drawn to the woman but you could feel a rhythm in the leaves around her, a sense of their motion. The whole picture was like drums beating.

Elizabeth woke at six in the morning and Tomas was gone like Zorro, her new friend. He'd left a note, *Thanks, see you tonight?* with a photograph of a person on a motorcycle that he'd pulled out of a larger picture and blown it up until it looked almost like a rubbed drawing, indefinite in its lines; it was the exact opposite of her sharp pictures, which made her laugh, and it had a few twenty dollar bills clipped to it. He'd cleaned up after himself but there was a lot of scrap paper in the garbage can.

○

She knew. She bloody well knew. When Heather walked into the house with the tall, handsome young man Barbara's radar went snaky. She held Heather tight, a bit longer than usual, both for the pleasant surprise of her daughter being there in her arms and also for time, to delay. She felt confused by the instinctive aversion snapping through her nervous system, and wanted time to gather herself together. Barbara smiled up at the young man—"Welcome"—and they shook hands. It was a new kind of presence for her. He put their bags down in the foyer. He was very polite, comfortable, all smiles and glad-to-meet-you-Mrs.-Carlyle, but he was a hollow child with the gift of appearance. He was accustomed to being looked at and being treated with particular interest for his appearance, one of those people others watched from across the room, across the street, from anywhere; there was always someone looking at him, and he could feel what they were thinking. Desire, envy. The Porsche driver was Narcissus, a movie star in the making, and he had somehow glommed onto Heather, no slouch herself, young Aphrodite. But this was an extreme case: the beauty of Aphrodite was somehow a reflection of the beauty of silvery Narcissus. This was something more than clothing, or framing. Her beauty was a contribution to his beauty and even the beauty of them together was his somehow, and so Heather became Echo.

The first morning, after Tomas returned from the photo lab, he and Marie joined Barbara in the kitchen nook for breakfast, planning how they would handle the day. They made the assumption that Munk would not show up in time. Barbara wondered whether they should call the police, and they decided to wait one more day. It was hard to imagine what the police would do. When they finished breakfast, Tomas brought Marie to the front window. "I want to show you something." Barbara followed them, curious. "Look." Tomas pointed out at the silver Porsche parked at the curb. "It has Ontario plates."

"Oh…" Marie spoke quietly, and took a long time before saying anything else, staring at the car, staying non-committal. She turned to Barbara. "Do you know whose car that is?"

"Yes. It belongs to Narcissus. My daughter's boyfriend. Is there something wrong?" It made complete sense to her that something would be wrong. She's been waiting to find out what that would be.

"No, I'm sure not. It must be a coincidence. We came across someone in a car like that around Lake Superior eleven days ago. We almost had an accident on the highway."

"He and Heather drove here from Calgary on Sunday, but I do know he's from Toronto. He's a movie actor. They're still sleeping upstairs, but I'm sure you'll meet him later."

Silvery Narcissus and young Aphrodite stretched their limbs out of the tangled sheets around ten in the morning. They let in the sunlight. Everyone else had left already and they had the house to themselves. They had coffee with blueberry scones. She told him more about the city, where they could shop later, and they talked about the rain. They showered together, flirty, they had sex in the shower. In the movie, we would have watched their bodies through the watery glass wall. They left the house and went downtown looking for clothes, something to do. He never said it out loud, but Narcissus was growing bored with Aphrodite. A week had passed and he was ready for another kind of adventure. Aphrodite could feel that displeasure growing in him and it hurt her feelings. She had never felt this before. She tried harder, though to be honest she was perfect, what else could she do? Who should she become? They sat in a bar in Gastown, the two of them with their stunning, numb smiles. Narcissus was filled with hope and myopia, his nervous system twitching to every person whose eyes turned their way. He'd already made up his mind that he would leave soon, but he did not tell her that yet. They agreed that they would drop by for the new exhibit that was opening at her mother's gallery—a photographer from Montreal, who was staying in the basement; Narcissus was interested in photography—and then they'd go out to a club. It was in a club that they had started together, and it seemed fitting that they would end the same way too.

Fine Examples

When Narcissus and Aphrodite arrived at the Carlyle Gallery that evening there were already seventy people in the room. For an exhibit by an unknown photographer from across the country, in those years before the internet, that was quite good. Barbara and Tomas were both pleased. Barbara knew almost everyone. Tomas knew almost no one, but strangers treated him with interest. The gallery wasn't big. The room felt crowded and there was a sense that something worthwhile was happening. Roy Kiyooka was there talking with a few friends. Earle Birney was there. Molly Bobak. Robert Creighton from the *Sun* was there; those people who gave the launch a sense of authenticity for others who recognized them. Everyone drinking wine, nibbling on cheese and hors d'oeuvres. Tomas and Marie were both busy, but they tried to keep an eye on people who were actually looking at the pictures, trying to gauge their reactions. Which pictures were they looking at? Did they spend some time with them?

When Narcissus and Aphrodite came into the room, everyone noticed, everyone turned to look and followed them for a moment with their eyes. They were either struck by the beauty of that woman and then the man beside her, or by the beauty of that man and then the woman. There was a kind of glowing aura about the couple. They seemed to hardly touch the ground, like ballet dancers holding their heads straight up over their supple spines, not pushing forward like the rest of us. This was all barely notable for them, just how it always was, but what did strike Narcissus was the idea that the crowd of people in the room, almost shoulder to shoulder, with drinks and in good spirits, were there because of photographs. Being a movie actor, their interest in pictures was something he could appreciate, it was his business too, after all, and he was curious to meet the photographer. *Is he famous?* It was possible that the photographer might like to take some pictures of him. He was always happy to have new headshots.

The photographer was wearing a nice blazer with a crisp white shirt and a paisley tie over a pair of jeans, though the tie was already loose around his neck. He'd had a haircut. His eyes were smiling, happy. Barbara had been introducing Tomas to everyone through the evening and he seemed to be enjoying himself. He received many compliments and he kept turning the conversation back to others. "I'm sorry, would you tell me your name again? What do you do? Are you a photographer too?" He spent quite a while with Elizabeth Mortimer-Lamb and her friends. He introduced Marie and told the group how his work had gone last night, that he had slept on a couch at the back of the gallery during the afternoon. He said that the show wouldn't even exist if it weren't for Elizabeth. They asked about Munk. They talked about the pictures. Some of the photographs already had discrete red dots on the cards next to them.

Sold.

Among the pictures on the walls there was one Marie had taken of herself in a hotel room mirror in Alberta. Tomas printed and framed the picture and called it *Red Dear*. He had used a marker to make a faint red line over one eye, which he thought was pretty humorous. In the picture Marie is holding the camera vertically, only a step or two away from the mirror. The viewer sees most of her face and her hands, her fingers, her right forearm, and the Minolta. Her sleeve is rolled up and slipping down to her elbow, along with a thin bracelet. The camera is in the centre of the picture, her face is to the left side. She'd been standing near a window and light comes to her from the left, half of her face in shadow. She is facing the mirror, serious. She is holding the camera away from her face but her eyes are looking at the viewfinder, not to the viewer. Her lips are closed. Because of the camera, you can only see part of her hair, a few strands curling over her forehead. She looks careful, studious. She is trying to take an accurate photograph. Once it was printed Marie found this picture too clever, but she did like the red line.

In the darkroom, Tomas had tried to formalize the exhibit. He manipulated the pictures, he cropped extravagantly, erasing signs of travel. He intended to remove the narrative traces, the snapshot, the travelogue, but the people in the gallery had all heard the story and they were adding in their own understanding and context.

Silvery Narcissus held young Aphrodite's hand while he looked at the pictures. What he saw was that most of the photographs were of one particular woman. He didn't know who she was but he understood that she was the root of the exhibit. She was the star of the show. When he was introduced to Tomas he was also introduced to Marie. He shook her hand. He offered his movie-star smile.

There were thirty-eight photographs on the walls. There were pictures of Marie, pictures of landscapes, pictures of birds, and as people slowly did the tour (the ones who hadn't just come for drinks), they all soon noticed her. The woman in the photographs was in the room with them; ordinary, but also not. She was wearing a dress the blue of eternity, the ultramarine sky. She wore jewellery, lapis earrings, soft, flat shoes (that she could scrunch into a backpack), lipstick, kohl and slight blue eyeshadow, like Cleopatra. They watched her, listened to her voice. Her presence suggested another world, the other side of the country. Narcissus studied her, watched how people treated her. People looked at Aphrodite but they kept turning back to Marie. She was the one they wanted to know more about, to know her. They read her gestures as though she was telling a story. She was a story. She and her husband had driven across the country on motorcycles that she had built herself, this woman who owned the room. They lost someone named Munk. They lost a whole other exhibit of framed colour photographs. People imagined what those other photographs were like. The vocabulary of images of a woman's body is infinite but as common as day. We have always been picturing the body of a woman in one way or another.

Marie and Tomas tried to circle around, working the room, judging people's reactions to the exhibit. The picture he most wanted them to see was one of the largest, horizontal, of Marie with the sky of birds behind her. The birds are not far and the way she's spread her arms accompanies the spread of their long wings. Her wingspan and theirs. Her arms are bare, her hair is tied in a ponytail, she is leaning forward slightly, as though she might duck her head, but she's turning up toward them too, watching, and you can see that she is laughing out loud. He watched people stand in front of this picture, how long they stood there. Did they talk? Mostly he stayed not far from Marie, always aware of each other, double-teaming. She had long fingers and short nails, rings, bracelets on her left wrist. Earrings, a cotton dress. She didn't know yet that she was pregnant.

Music was playing quietly, recordings of small chamber groups. Barbara had given considerable time to the selection, but the people were noisy and no one really heard the music. It was just there, ignored, string quartets, violins, cello, viola—Barbara's favourite—and every once in a while she threw in a recording of a Phillip Glass composition, which had become another favourite. She had recently seen *Einstein on the Beach* in New York City with her husband and she was in awe. She found the sections choreographed by Lucinda Childs especially thrilling, the music and the way the dancers moved was hypnotic, and she played the music this evening, eager to see how people would respond. Would they be hypnotized? But tonight the music was for a stationary audience, well-dressed. She had wine served, there were nibblies, there was music, flowers on two stands, one bouquet was from Michael, who couldn't be there that evening, Tomas's pictures on the wall, and so many people in the room. She could breathe. She could sigh. When she smiled you could see Heather's beauty in her. What an odd custom, she thought fleetingly, to invite a hundred people to a gallery to show them photographs they have never seen before, that you think they will find interesting, and then serve them food and drink while they stand around in clusters chatting with each other, with their backs to the pictures. Why serve them anything? Why don't they just come quietly and look at the pictures? Though they did buy eleven photographs that evening.

After the first hour Barbara could let herself relax. She joined Tomas and Marie for a moment, happy with the evening. She called Heather and her boyfriend to come over, and introduced everyone. "Narcissus is the fellow who owns that silver Porsche." Barbara turned to him. "Marie was asking about your car." She was dying to see what would happen, too curious to wait until later.

Narcissus smiled. He misunderstood, started talking about the Porsche, how much he liked driving it. How much Heather liked it too, didn't she? Low to the ground and fast. He could show it to them if they'd like, he could take them for a ride. His mind was working fast, watching Marie but checking the others too, trying not to be obvious, which he was. She was older that he was, but there was something about her that he was drawn to, she was attractive, and she was staying in the same house that he and Heather were. He was already thinking he'd stay another day or two.

"We passed someone in a car like yours in Northern Ontario about ten days ago."

He smiled. "Yes, that could have been me. I don't remember, but I was driving around Lake Superior at that time. I'd just finished a film shoot; we were making a movie about Tom Thomson. You know, the painter?"

"Do you remember getting into a sort of race on the highway with two motorcycles?"

He laughed again, pointed. "Was that you?"

"You nearly killed me, you fucking asshole!" She stepped closer and Tomas followed, the hair rising on the back of their necks.

Barbara stepped in front of Narcissus, afraid. *Oh my God, they're going to fight.*

Heather pulled at her boyfriend's arm. "What's going on?"

Narcissus was talking fast. He put on his best voice. He apologized, though he also shook his head, *No.* "You were never in danger," he said. "I know how to drive." But then he apologized again. "I'm really sorry. I thought we were just fooling around, having fun. It's boring up there."

Barbara was holding Marie's hand, pulled her back a

few steps. She knew that if Marie calmed down, Tomas would too. Other people were watching, turning, wanting to meet them, curious to see what was going on. "Why don't we talk about this later at home?"

○

Marie and Tomas stayed in Barbara's basement for two more days, one of which they spent sightseeing. They drove around Stanley Park, Brockton Point, Prospect Point, and ate lunch by English Bay. They cruised downtown. They leaned on a railing looking down at Granville Island, but didn't go there. On the second day they stayed at the house gathering their energies in the garden. Marie was almost healed. She worked on the bikes. Tomas was passing tools and reading maps out loud; they had planned to return through the United States, and after experiencing the first half of the trip, they talked about distances, finding ways to shorten each day's drive. They had fourteen days to get home, to be back at work on day fifteen. *Easy peasy.* They drank tea in lawn chairs trying to count the bees in the flowers, trying to spot the nest. Later in the afternoon, when it was especially sunny and warm, dry for a while now that they were leaving, and while Barbara was still at work, they pummelled the Porsche driver a little bit in the space near the well. By this time Heather was fine with whatever happened to him. Aloof, like Aphrodite. She was surprised at how quickly the fight escalated, one minute and it exploded. He had come outside, all charm for Marie, good-looking, standing close.

He said something but she pushed him. And then he raised his hand, acting tough, and that was all it took. They were on him, both of them. The reality of people's anger set Heather's nervous system on high alert, though the truth is that after the first moments she was more concerned for her mother's garden than for Narcissus. "Watch out for the rhododendrons!" she cried. She did apologize afterward for saying that, laughing and touching him like a teenage girl. "My mother would have been really pissed." And she helped Narcissus pack his bag and go. He was still very attractive; nothing would change that. They kissed goodbye. "This has been nice." He looked rougher now, tougher. Narcissus mentioned to Heather more than once that there had been two of them and only one of him. In the evening, Heather joined Marie and Tomas to take Barbara out to dinner. They told her about the fight in the backyard, and apologized. Marie was especially troubled with herself, *how did that happen*, astonished and guilty, but Tomas felt it could have been worse. Barbara was happy enough that the Porsche driver was gone and Heather had stayed.

They left the house early the following morning. Marie padded around in her bare feet and a Harley shirt, she started coffee and Tomas roused himself a few minutes later. They had a shower together, coffee, bread and cheese, cleaned up, and left a thank-you note for Barbara. Tomas already had a cheque for the first sales, and Barbara felt she would sell most of the other photographs. Tomas said he would be sure to spread the word about how much he liked the Carlyle Gallery.

The others were just waking up as Marie and Tomas were getting ready to leave, going back and forth, packing the bikes, tying everything down. The sun was coming up but the air was still cool and the garden was dewy-sweet. They had lists of cities going through their minds. *I've been everywhere…* They picked up their helmets and checked in with each other, *a kiss for the start of a trip*, that nice feeling. The engines were smooth, right, ready to go. They drove carefully along the path through the trellis, feet down but trying to keep their boots out of the garden, and turned into the lane. Tomas pulled the gate shut behind them.

In Memory of Mary Griffin Hannan
1913–1956

Acknowledgements

Thank you to Guy Birchard, Ian Ferrier, Katrina Hucal, Molly Shea-Hannan, Ryan Van Huistjee, and Kevin Williams. Thank you to Katia Grubisic, who edited this book. I am grateful for her influence.

The title is from the book *By Grand Central Station I Sat Down and Wept* by Elizabeth Smart. Reprinted by permission of HarperCollins Publishers Ltd. Copyright © 1945, 2015, the estate of Elizabeth Smart.

The epigraph is from *The Handbook of Disappointed Fate*, by Anne Boyer (Ugly Duckling Press, 2018) used with the permission of Anne Boyer.

For more on Maurice Maeterlinck, or for a quite wonderful book on bees, I suggest *The Hive: The Story of the Honeybee and Us,* by Bee Wilson (Thomas Dunne Books, 2004).

For more on Eadweard Muybridge, I suggest *River of Shadows: Eadweard Muybridge and the Technological Wild West*, by Rebecca Solnit (Viking Penguin, 2003).